Dearly Deported
Return of the People of the Sun

Edmundo Osorio

Library of Congress Control Number 2013905390

www.eddieoradio.com

Table of Contents

Preface

I had been living in Tijuana, Baja California, Mexico, for eight years and commuting to the United States on a daily basis. Because my children adapted so well and loved Mexico, I decided to stay; during that time I met many of their friends. It appeared that every English-speaking deportee into Tijuana befriended my three sons, who were well known in the neighborhood as *Los Gringos* (The Americans) because they spoke fluent English and attended school in America. Many of these young men had been thugs in their respective "hoods" back home in the USA. Most were tattooed up as if to scream "Hey, look at me! I want you to notice me; arrest me!" Everyone I met, however, was very respectful, and no one ever crossed me.

This book was written during the first week of 2013. While nursing the worst flu I ever had, I couldn't sleep one night and the whole idea came at me in half-dreams. The next morning when I went to work, I was loopy from the lack of sleep and the remnants of flu symptoms. Before the lunch hour, my sister e-mailed me that my 19-year-old nephew, Victor, had been killed in a car crash, a day before New Year's Eve.

I couldn't believe it; I was heartbroken and hurt inside, thinking of my cousin Martha and what she must have been going through. I imagined my own son, my youngest, who was the same age; I was overcome with emotion. I went home after my shift, e-mailed my boss and told him I would be taking the next 10 days off. I began to write the entire story that had haunted my dreams the night before; it was my own way of grieving. I prayed to God to work through me, through my hands, to inspire me, to touch my soul. God responded, as he always does; it all started coming together.

I remembered the deportees' sad stories, their trials and tribulation; their tales of deportation were fascinating to me. My eldest son, who by 2012 had formed his own freestyle rap group, inspired the idea to write a collection of rap lyrics about guys who had lived most of their lives in America and were deported to Mexico. He quickly dismissed the lyrics I wrote as not his style (however, I would find snippets of them peppered in all of his songs when he performed at our home on Saturday nights with his two younger brothers). I wrote a whole set of lyrics, enough to fill an album for my son that I would call Dearly Deported. I designed the front of the album with the title in Old English, a' la Cypress Hill.

The reason I took the time to develop this book was to bring attention to, and put a face on, the new breed of deportee, one who is never shown on television and has created a whole new dynamic in the border region. These are people like you and me; everyday people who you would never suspect were brought here illegally as kids and have grown up with that stigma. They could be your neighbor, your mechanic or your neighborhood grocer; the face of stereotypical undocumented migrants has adapted to an ever-changing system.

I had never written a book like this in my life; everything I wrote was either for business or comedy. I had published cartoons and written two slapstick comedy movie scripts that I never published or released to the public. I hope to finish editing both and release them soon, God willing.

Edmundo Osorio

6

Introduction

They are all around us, the invisible People of the Sun. They wash our cars and wash our clothes; they cook and serve our food. They groom our manicured lawns, they clean our houses and babysit our children. They pick the fruits and vegetables that we eat, from the fields and orchards. We trust them with our daily lives and we depend on their continuous loyal service. They listen to our constant complaints about our First World problems; they listen patiently and only when we ask will they talk back with a classic response: "*Si, patron.*" ("Yes, boss.")

They are the undocumented workforce that has woven itself into the very fabric of the American quilt. They could never be extracted as proposed by some, unless you want to disrupt life as we know it. They are the good, the bad, the seen and the unseen; you run across their handiwork on any given day, seven days a week.

Theirs is a roller-coaster life full of ups and downs and a feeling that any day may get caught, and unlike most of their American counterparts, they live each day as if it will be their last in America. They walk with eyes in the backs of their heads. They come from many countries: Guatemala, El Salvador, Honduras, Venezuela, Cuba, Dominican Republic, China, Iran, Armenia, even Canada, but the majority come from America's neighbor to the south, Mexico.

An effort must be made to achieve a semblance of immigration control, so we find a few here, some more there; we huddle these poor and weak masses together and send them back to the places from whence they came. They are but a tiny fraction of the whole, yet they are enough to keep the natives from becoming restless and keep the politicians in office.

Many of the recently deported aliens have spent more time in America than in their own countries, and they speak fluent English as their only language, especially if they arrived here as children. Some don't even understand their own native tongue.

They are very resourceful and hardworking people but can be volatile at times, which renders them exploitable. So when they get the shock of deportation to a country they hardly know, it is a severe blow and yet another setback in their struggle to get ahead. If they adapt to life in Mexico, Guatemala, El Salvador or wherever else they came from, it won't be as lucrative as the *Jaula de Oro* -- or golden cage -- of a life they had in America. Some have skills, but most are just hardworking folk. A few are entrepreneurs, sellers of both the legal and the illegal. Whether at swap meets or back alleys, they peddle their goods.

Many young thugs get deported after serving time for crimes they committed in the name of gang violence. They end up in Mexican border towns such as Tijuana, Ciudad Juarez, Piedras Negras, Matamoros or Nogales. Tattooed, with shaven heads, and possessing drug-peddling skills and street smarts, they will either survive on the street, speaking a hybrid form of Spanglish mixed with Pachuco, or get arrested right from the get-go at the revolving door. Worse, they might end up dead at their final destination.

Dedication

This book is dedicated to God, my father in heaven, and to Luis, my father on earth, who have always been there for me at every step of the way, shown me patience and compassion, guided me, counseled me, helped me get back up when I fell, and pushed me forward on my way again. If seven times I fell from grace, seven times I was forgiven.

The Package

In a little town in Mexico along the Baja California border with California, a heavyset man sat in the back room of a chapel, a portable mobile office like the kind used on construction sites. An old typewriter sat on the sturdy desk in front of him; the typewriter was loaded with a sheet of paper titled "Journey of Souls; Adventures of a Bohemian Spirit: Chapter Twenty Two." The older, balding man muttered some words in Spanish. A Tijuana tabloid newspaper, which had been opened to the Crime section, lay on the desk to the left of the typewriter. There was a picture of a gang of armed men who were arrested following a cartel-style shootout in downtown Tijuana; some of the men had tattooed faces and necks.

There was a name in the article, circled in red; "RIP" had been scribbled next to the circle. The man looked over at the article and shook his head. He picked up an open letter addressed to him that he had opened previously. Inside the letter was a photograph which made him smile; he sighed. The photograph was a Polaroid of five guys in a marijuana field clowning around with two pit bull dogs.

With his elbows on the desktop, he intertwined his fingers, put his hands against his forehead, and began to pray. His head was down. As he prayed silently, he gripped his hands together tighter as he began to sway back and forth as if the more he rocked the stronger his prayer became.

After a few minutes his head flew up, his eyes looking to the ceiling. Tears were rolling down his face. He then took a deep breath and placed the palms of his hands on the desktop. He exhaled into a deep, satisfying, peaceful, state and sat quietly for a few seconds.

He looked at the article on the desk once more, and began typing away; he typed nonstop for hours. He looked outside through the windows and sat there a minute in a wonder. The green leaves on the trees danced in the breeze gracefully, like a flock of birds flying through the air.

There was a tattered, dog-eared Bible, with yellow sticky notes stuck onto layer upon layer of pages. It sat to the right of him, on top of two inches of typed pages. A coffee mug, half-filled with cold coffee, sat on top of a set of blueprints that were laid across a table behind him.

The wall to the right of the entry was cluttered with children's drawings, pictures of people in the community, all types of crosses made out of plastic, wood, and plaster. A framed degree from the University of Baja California hung next to the clutter, along with other citations and awards. A white dry erase board was on the wall next to it; an intensive scribbling covered the board as a testament to a deep lecture in faith, Aztec research and community involvement. It was all that was left of a jam session earlier in the day.

The main wall was adorned with pictures and sculptures in bas relief of ancient Aztec codices, Aztec calendars, pictures of Aztec warriors, ancient Mesoamerican maps, photographs of Aztec pyramids, shaman masks, feathers and articles, new and old, as if an Aztec researcher's work in progress was slowly taking shape.

On the left side was a bookshelf that took up the entire wall. There were books about theology, ancient books in English and Spanish. There were many books about Aztecs, the Maya, Toltecs, Olmecs – any and every kind of book that would surely qualify one as an expert in all things Mesoamerican, if one read them all.

Towards the back of the room there was a cot with a neatly tucked blanket and pillow. Someone had placed folded clothes on top, as if it had not been slept in for a while. The cot was a sign of late-night study sessions. A squeaky fan turned above the man, giving him a slight warm breeze.

The phone rang. He answered it and spoke to the person on the other end. He gave them the address to the temple. "Yes, just tell the cab driver that I will pay for the fare when you arrive, don't worry about it. It will be good to see you again. Yes, they are here, they arrived yesterday. Uh huh. Yes, the man of the hour is here too, but he's looked better, bless his soul. Yeah, it was hard, but I was able to get hold of her, she got married, that's why I couldn't locate her. Yes, I am so glad you sent me the backpack or none of this would have been possible; let me tell you it's going to be the most beautiful service. Yes. Yes, okay, see you soon!" He finally finished with the caller in Spanish. He hung up the phone with a satisfied smile; the caller had put him in a good mood.

He continued to write like a man who had a lot of things to say; sometimes he would laugh to himself, or get teary eyed. Other times he would ask a question and then proceed to answer it himself out loud, but during this time he never stopped writing. When he finally stopped, it was only to stretch his legs; he took a walk in the beautiful climate, a climate that was good for his soul. He didn't like to drive; he was accustomed to walking whenever possible.

As he walked down the quiet street some cars passed by. The occupants honked and waved, he waved back. People who passed him on the sidewalk stopped to talk and ask him questions; he patiently spoke to all of them. A raggedy young man, recently deported, approached him and gave him a long-winded story; the big man pointed towards the chapel, took out a business card, scribbled something on the back, and gave the guy a pat on the back. The young man continued on to the temple. After walking for an hour, or about four miles, he was back at his office. He returned to his place on the chair in front of the typewriter.

Mexington

A sign leading into a small Nebraska town read, "Welcome to Lexington, Nebraska" Somebody had crossed out the "L" and replaced it with an "M" – that's how it was referred to by the young Hispanic residents: Mexington. Cars zigzagged in and out of a predominantly Latino commercial zone known as Little Mexico. It was riddled with buyers and sellers, like a giant outdoor swap meet, or *tianguis*. A stereo store was blasting music: *Hecho En Mexico* (Made in Mexico) by *Quinto Sol* (Fifth Sun).

Lowriders cruised by the side street; some hopped up and down, others side to side, and still another in a three-wheel motion. Street performers dressed as Aztec shamans performed ritual dances for money, they would clean your aura and get rid of any hexes put on you; a fire breather spewed out streams of fire from his mouth like a flamethrower in a Vietnam jungle. Jugglers and acrobats delighted the crowd as food vendors meandered around with every sort of Mexican delicacy imaginable.

A food stand would make you a *vampiro* (vampire) from scratch. A new favorite dish made famous in Mexicali, B.C., Mexico, it consisted of a fresh baked corn *tortilla*, made from kneaded *masa*, that had been overcooked on a hot *comal* until it warped to a perfectly toasted crunchy disc. Grated Monterey Jack cheese was added, and as the cheese melted, choice diced cuts of grilled *carne asada* were toppled on until they melted together. More cheese was added. It was then topped with chopped onion, tomatoes, cilantro and homemade salsa. Served with an ice cold Mexican Coca Cola in a green tinted glass bottle, it was as original as any of the offerings at *Chicali's* (Mexicali's) finest food stands.

Across the way, a man had a colorful horse buggy with a harnessed white donkey that had been painted with black stripes like a zebra, the kind typically found in Tijuana, Mexico: a zonkey. A picture of the family would run five dollars. Next to that stall was a tannery, a seller of all things leather; Mexican imports. The hottest item on his racks was the *huarache* sandals made with used tires as soles and leather uppers, shipped from the Tapatio city of Guadalajara in Jalisco, Mexico.

For twenty dollars you could buy an authentic Jerga pullover hoodie, made from hemp that would last forever; one could haggle with the salesman and lower the price to twelve dollars. There were also authentic striped *zarapes* (cloth ponchos) and *sombreros* (straw cowboy hats). If you were decorating your living room and wanted a classy piece of furnishing, there were many velvet paintings to choose from: Elvis and Jesus, dogs playing poker, matadors, dogs shooting pool, or unicorns – you could even get a classy Ron Burgundy, whatever your choice of décor.

It looked like a modern-day Tenochtitlan marketplace; all that was missing was the great Aztec temple. Young men dressed in saggy jeans and baggy shirts break-danced in synchronization to a hip hop song in Spanish; anything and everything was for sell or trade. A hustling and bustling, a new type of commerce, welcoming the dawn of a new era.

The newly arrived Hispanic population had engrained itself in its new city, like their ancient ancestors once did when the people of Aztlan left the land of the north, their native land, trekked down south to Central Mexico, and arrived in the Valley of Anahuac, changing history forever. This was the opposite. These people had left their homeland to come north and settle in a new, prosperous land.

Down the road, outside of Little Mexico, a rare sight: An immigration pickup had detained three young men outside a bar for causing a disturbance. *"Come se llama?"* asked an officer to a young dark man with bleached highlights in his shoulder-length hair. *"Yeyo,"* said the diminutive teen.
"Your real name?" the officer asked in Spanish. "Ruben... Ruben Sanchez," the teen replied; that was not his real name.

"Do you have an identification card, any papers?" the officer asked in Spanish. Yeyo told him he forgot his wallet at home, but when the officer searched him, he found a white nylon tri-fold wallet, the kind with a Velcro closing. A black Nirvana logo was emblazoned on the front. The officer figured the obvious and loaded him into the bed of the pickup along with the other two, who were bloodied from fighting with each other, much to Yeyo's misfortune; he'd tried, in vain, to stop them. They were kicked out of the bar, the cops were called. The cops, upon evaulating the scenario, had called immigration.

Yeyo sat in the back of the pickup, his long hair blowing. He had his head down, against the direction of the wind. He was wearing just a T shirt. He was cold, so he wrapped his arms around himself to keep warm. He'd been at the bar interviewing for the guitar player position when his buddy had gotten into a fight with another patron. Yeyo was sad that he had missed his chance, but dismissed it as he had the other dozen times. He started to think about his first audition, in El Salvador, in a notoriously dangerous bar located on the border with Guatemala. It was open mic night.

He remembered so vividly, the emcee introducing him. He felt amazing, like a star. He began strumming to Nirvana's "All Apologies." He began to sing, spot-on exactly like Kurt Cobain. His eyes were closed; he never noticed that the audience, not interested in a loud rock song from a foreign land, was not paying attention. They were talking and laughing among themselves. One drunken customer threw a bottle that narrowly missed Yeyo's head and smashed against the back wall. Yeyo never noticed. "We want to hear *El Chuntaro y Los Tres Huastecos!*" screamed the drunk in Spanish.

The song wound down. Yeyo didn't understand English, nor did he have any idea what he was singing; he'd searched for the lyrics on the web in an El Salvadoran Internet cafe. He did, however, understand the spirit of the song, that universal, deep, soulful spirit we all possess, the power to decode the mysteries of the universe.

A performance appreciated by only two or three people in a bar full of about 50 rowdy Salvadorans, some partying on their last night before going to El Norte, into Guatemala. They were the ones who referred to themselves as *"tres veces mojados,"* or three-time wetbacks.

When Salvadorans enter illegally into Guatemala, they will be wetbacks in that country. If they are successful, they will attempt to traverse the Guatemalan landscape and take a shot at entering into Mexico, also as illegals, rendering them wetbacks a second time; finally, if they can get through the treacherous Mexican territory – a gauntlet of dangers navigated successfully by only a small percentage of people – they can attempt the mother of all illegal crossings: the entry into the United States of America. If they make it into the United States alive they will have attained that ever-elusive title of three-time wetback, which may sound derogatory to some, but to them is a crown.

Songs have been written about the three-time wetback, resilient, hardworking men and women who risk their lives not just for the dollar, but for the opportunity to live in a country that not only preaches truth, justice, and equality to all, but actually practices it, for the most part. You cannot be a coward, lazy, a complainer, nor afraid of hard labor and be a three-time wetback. No, you must strive to better your life and the lives all who depend on you. You must have as much faith in God as Moses, knowing that He will deliver you to the Promised Land, the land of milk and honey.

The entire scenario is reminiscent of the baby sea turtles that hatch on the beach by the hundreds of thousands and try to make it to the awaiting waves of the ocean, where they will find freedom from land predators. However, many are picked off by seagulls or other birds, or even people who poach or are just curious. Some have trouble crawling on the sand with their clumsy flippers and are beaten down by the sun, drawing their last breath before they reach the water. Either way, they have a high mortality rate. Only a tiny fraction actually makes it to the sea, where they will face many more enormous threats until they reach adulthood.

The irony is that although, in modern times, borders divide these nations, the people of three of these countries, five including Honduras and Belize, were all part of the same Aztec Empire. Interestingly enough, indigenous people may have traversed the same routes 500 years ago, embarking on the same journey north – at that time as courageous warriors instead of illegal migrants hiding in the dark and afraid for their lives.

Yeyo walked off the stage never knowing if they liked him or not, but never caring either; he sang and played because it was in his soul, he could not live without it. He had come up north from a little pueblo in southern El Salvador to escape the violence and pressure from the gangs that were threatening him back home.

Tres Veces Mojado – Three-Time Wetback

In the bed of the pickup, as Yeyo reflected on his misfortune, he muttered to himself, *"Chinga su madre."* He remembered that he left his guitar back at the bar. He thought about asking the immigration officer if he could go back, then realized how naively absurd that must sound. As the wind blew in his face, it reminded him of sitting atop that train, the train of death.

The trip began the day after the audition, when he realized that maybe that venue was not ready for his music. He was with Paco, a friend he'd met in the El Salvador border town. Yeyo had a knack for making friends anywhere; this new friend had crossed before and would be his guide crossing into Guatemala and into Mexican territory. Paco knew the routes and could take him as far as Arriaga, Chiapas, where Paco would be picking up his uncle and taking him back to El Salvador. There, Yeyo could hop onto the train of death and gamble on his wits, blessings from heaven, and sheer luck.

The crossing into Guatemala from El Salvador was no problem; they simply walked two miles east of the San Cristobal border crossing and walked right in under an old rusty barbed wire fence. That wasn't to say that there was no danger involved. The Guatemalan farmers were in constant patrol for wandering illegal Salvadoran immigrants trying to steal some resources for their trip up north. They were tired of being ripped off and were more than willing to put some lead shot from their shotguns into the asses of any illegals who trespassed.

Yeyo and Paco traversed the side roads out of sight, trying to melt into the local population, Yeyo's six-string strapped to his back. Guatemala wasn't as dangerous as Mexico would be, but it still caused Yeyo concern. He remembered hearing stories of young men being taken prisoner and made into sex slaves, or being shipped to other countries as slaves, or getting beaten and killed in some demonic ritual.

Guatemala still had many who practiced what they called White Magic or *Santeria* – it was all over the place, especially in the seedy areas among those who participated in illegal activities, and there were many would practice some sort of witchery, a witchery that sometimes required a human sacrifice.

When they reached the border crossing at Tecun Uman, Guatemala, which crossed into Ciudad Hidalgo, Chiapas, Mexico, near the city of Tapachula, Mexico, things got a bit trickier. Now the Mexicans wanted nothing to do with illegals from their southern borders. Mexicans wanted the U.S. border and the American Dream all to themselves.

They followed other illegal migrants to the western shore, where they noticed them making a deal with a local fisherman. After the money was exchanged, the migrants and their leader got into a panga boat. Obviously, Paco and Yeyo had to do the same.

Yeyo was a little short on the payment to his panga captain, but the captain was more than happy to take the guitar off his hands. "You'll surely lose that in the water, you don't need it, boy!" the captain remarked in Spanish. Yeyo had lost guitars in the past, once in his hometown when a bar owner took his guitar after he found out Yeyo was underage.

Yeyo had left most of his earnings, money to be used for his passage, at home with his sister. His plan was to call her and have her wire the money he needed. That was the best way to avoid getting all his money taken away by coyotes, police, taxers or con artists. The landscape was thick with these types, and seldom did anyone traverse that territory without running into one, two, or every one of these opportunists.

Yeyo and Paco were always on the lookout and kept their distance from other illegal migrants heading north, practically tracking their every move. They knew that they would be better off following the other migrants from afar, and if those people fell into danger, then

Yeyo and Paco could avoid the same outcome by taking a different route. They dared not be seen by the illegal migrants ahead of them, or the leader would surely flay them. They walked and trekked for hours and days. They mainly crept along Highway 200, which headed to Arriaga, Yeyo's goal.

Arriaga was where Yeyo could board the train that carried freight and illegal migrants by the hundreds. The train engineers were well aware of this, but there was nothing they could do. Sometimes they colluded with local mobsters and delivered a fresh load of illegal migrants to awaiting coffee farmers to use as indentured servants. The farmers housed and fed the migrants and charged them exorbitant rates for food and lodging, letting them work it off. They never could achieve that, because the debt added up so quickly.

They arrived on foot at Arriaga, Chiapas, where Yeyo would board the train to Mexico City, an 800-mile journey on the train of death, with the final destination of Ixtepec, Oaxaca. Paco and Yeyo said their goodbyes. Paco had to return; he had completed his mission without a hitch.

When the train, which was loaded with corn, minerals, fuel in its tankers, and other commodities, left the cargo station, it began slowly chugging away, and illegal migrants jumped out of every nook and cranny, out of bushes and trees, out of manholes and crates, and began hopping onto the train like fleas onto a furry dog.

As the migrants ran and jumped onto the moving train, Yeyo could hear the screams of people falling under the wheels of the train. Some didn't get a good handle, or the handle they had meant to grab was taken by a quicker person. One man, holding tight, was pulled by his shirt by somebody who had lost footing and grabbed at him; they both fell under and were crushed to death by the iron wheels of death.

Some who could not run fast enough or climb quickly enough hopped onto the open railcars with cattle or sheep being transported.

These were the worst areas, since the riders were victimized easier and spotted faster, not to mention that the railcars smelled awful; it was hot and humid. The coyotes would find these migrants first and tax them, a true taxation without representation. Yeyo had successfully avoided these coyotes. He had come this far by being two steps ahead every time, and of course, he'd been lucky.

Yeyo climbed to the top of the rail car. He found a spot that was vented for the cattle, and it was six inches below the surface of the railcar – a perfect bed for the night's travel, he thought. One kid who could have been his own brother asked Yeyo if he wanted to hear music, the *Guerreros de Metal – Te Pareces Tanto a Mi*. They each listened to an ear bud. One kept forward watch and the other looked back. They formed an unspoken bond.

Yeyo was amazed that he had been so lucky and was sure that God was on his side. The sun had gone down, and the other young man had already fallen asleep. Yeyo saw that all the migrants were sleeping and the night was coming; he hunkered down in his makeshift bed and slept.

Yeyo awakened to a horrible sound, the sound of heads cracking and bones busting. People were yelling and crying, but it was dark and they could not see. It was pandemonium in the dark. A low bridge had taken out many people who had not crouched down enough. One quarter of the migrants had been crushed by a metal overpass. A terrified Yeyo could only cover his ears and pray; he prayed hard, like he'd never prayed before. It was the first time in his trip that he had really been frightened; he began to cry.

The next morning, a nightmare awakened him. He dreamed that his *madrecita* had fallen off the train and was calling to him, "*Yeyo, Yeyo, ayudame* (help me)." Yeyo got up quickly. The sun was coming up on the eastern horizon. Blood was on the surface of the train roof, bodies spread around, people still asleep. His new friend was no longer there; he knew the train would be making a stop and the taxers, coyotes, or police would be coming to tax or arrest them.

He heard someone call him; it was his newfound friend already climbing down.

They jumped off one half-mile before the next town. They started to run so that they could board the train again. This was how they would avoid getting caught, arrested, or taxed and sent to the coffee plantations, where they would be paid three dollars and fifty cents a day but charged four dollars a day for room and board. They would be slaves to a system that would never let them leave; no one would ever find them.

Yeyo and his newfound friend ran as fast as they could. They were very much alike in stature and spirit, happy-go-lucky types who seemed to be content with music. They arrived at the outskirts of the train depot. They kept running. Their eyes were fixed ahead, but they knew the taxers were all around. Their speed was their best asset; people couldn't tax what they couldn't catch, the young men figured.

They waited behind some bushes where other local migrants had gathered. There were many women and children; they crouched very low trying to not stand out. As the train approached, it was still slow enough as it was leaving the depot; the boarding of illegals began all over again. He climbed that train like a 5-year-old on a jungle gym. People were screaming and crying, falling off; women fell to the dirt, their mouths filled with blood and dirt as they unsuccessfully tried to hop aboard the train, which was too high a jump for them.

Yeyo felt sorry for them, but self-preservation was the only attribute that would get him to America. He looked around for his friend, but the young man was nowhere in sight. As Yeyo looked back, he saw that his friend was being held by some local thugs along with other migrants. Police were around them as well. Yeyo was sad for his friend, but they both had spoken about the consequences of their trek. Like popcorn kernels, some popped, some didn't.

The train arrived at the Mexico City outskirts, where Yeyo again did an early bail from the train of death. He made the sign of the cross and kissed the ground. His most dreaded deed was now behind him, but he still needed to get himself to the U.S. border, which was across almost 500 miles of dangerous Mexican terrain. He went to a local café where he found a telegraph office; he called home and had a family member wire money for the next leg of his trip. He ate a meal, bought a change of clothes, stayed overnight at a cheap hotel and prepared for his final journey to America.

Yeyo's plan was to take a bus to Tampico, Tamaulipas, where he would either hitch hike or get a boat ride to the border. The young Salvadoran was a clean-shaven, non-threatening skinny fella with bleached hair that went down to his shoulders. His appearance allowed him to meld within any atmosphere. He got onto a bus in Mexico City; the bus was headed to Tamaulipas. On the bus he befriended a young college girl who went by Loly. She was heading home to stay with her parents for the summer. She was attending school at a prestigious university in Mexico City; her major was music. She had a fear of flying.

They talked for hours all the way to Tampico, where she was going to be picked up by her cousin. From there, they would drive to her home in Matamoros. She was fluent in English. He made her laugh. He confessed his illegal status and his admiration for anything American, including English speakers; he yearned to speak and understand the English language. She thought him a country bumpkin, but she liked him for that reason. She offered him safe passage to the border; he accepted.

They were picked up at the Tampico bus depot by Loly's female cousin, Mila, who drove a new convertible. Mila lived in Tampico, but she had agreed to drive up the coast and stay the summer at Loly's house. They drove with the top down; a road trip Mexican style. Mila motioned to Loly, then made a comment and pointed towards the glove box. Loly opened the glove box, took out a marijuana joint and said in Spanish, "I've been dying for a hit the whole way!" She pushed in the car's cigarette lighter to activate it, which quickly popped out cherry red hot. She lit the joint, which she puffed and enjoyed like someone having her last cigarette in front of a firing squad.

"You want a hit?" She passed it towards the back to Yeyo. Yeyo had never smoked any drug or cigarette, but didn't want to offend these nice ladies, so he pretended to hit the joint before going into violent, convulsing coughs; the girls laughed and continued to finish the joint. A few hours later they arrived at Loly's house, Yeyo was amazed at the sprawling ranch. This was no ordinary house; this was a house of a very important person. Loly told him her father was in the export business; both girls laughed at the comment.

They showed Yeyo inside and introduced him to her father, a big, tough-looking man who frightened Yeyo. Yeyo, almost trembling, shook the man's hand. In Spanish, the man said, "Any friend of my little girl is a friend of mine. My daughter says you are on your way to America. I have business up there, in Nebraska. I could help you." He winked, and then gave Yeyo a big bear hug.

The Prom Queen

With a GPA of 4.7, she was selected as valedictorian at her high school, an honors student with straight A's since elementary school; she carried a schedule full of Advanced Placement classes. She'd been captain of the varsity volleyball squad since freshman year, and was voted Most Likely to Succeed by her class. A poster child for success, she was a classic overachiever.

Her long, athletic legs enhanced her bronze skin and big black eyes. She was a natural beauty who never wore makeup. She didn't have to, yet she was always accused of wearing mascara or lip liner; a trait inherited from her Aztec roots.

Nelly, as they called her, was anything but the Aztec princess for whom she'd been named. She could be tougher than most guys when she needed to be, and she needed to be often, since she'd been placed with a host family when she was 8 years old.

Her somewhat crooked smile was more like a sculptor's flaw, which added an indefinable hook that drove guys crazy. She was nominated for Prom Queen and won by a landslide; the world was hers for the taking, and she was not going to stop until she was accepted into Harvard Law School. There was one little tiny problem. Actually, it was a huge problem, a secret nobody knew.

It was Thursday, after graduation, and Nelly was at the mall bookstore. She was wearing a pink Class of 2012 belly shirt and pink shorts, with matching Converse All Stars. She answered her phone. "Nelly, we're going to the Repeal SB1070 rally at the Phoenix City Hall. We want you to come with us." It was her friend Darlene. Nelly was uncomfortable and tried to weasel her way out, but her friend insisted. "Come on, it will be fun. You already missed Senior Ditch Day, we can be rebels today all in the name of our brothers and sisters from south of the border."

Darlene was Nelly's best friend. "Where are you?" Darlene inquired. "I'm at the mall. I was with Catalina but she met up with Bart, I think she bailed on me," responded Nelly.

"I'll be there in 15 minutes." Sure enough, Darlene was there in 14. Nelly got inside Darlene's new silver convertible Volkswagen and they drove towards downtown Phoenix; Nelly was a little nervous but excited at the same time. Nelly was not one for a spontaneous rendezvous, especially of the notorious kind.

Everything in Nelly's life was regimented so as to get the most out every second of every minute of every day. She had never been in trouble one day in her life. When they arrived within sight of City Hall, they were both amazed at the throngs of people. It was like the '60s all over again, or what they perceived as the '60s from the films and books they saw and read.

People were protesting a change to immigration law; they were the youth, the future, they were going to change the world for the better. There was electricity in the air; they were both caught up in the excitement of the crowd. Were they witnessing history? Either way, it was an experience that would add to their youthful memories, giving them depth of soul; this might have been something Harvard would like, a young, smart female minority overachiever ready to change the world.

As they walked, they were absorbed into the crowd and were handed picket signs. "Repeal SB1070! Repeal SB1070! Repeal SB1070!" they chanted as they marched, locked elbow to elbow. They were from all walks of life: young, old, brown, black, white, yellow, rich, poor, educated, uneducated.

They were the grassroots of the society, and they were exercising their civil rights. As they got closer to City Hall, she saw them: armed uniformed officers in riot gear. Some were mounted on horses, all were very menacing.

Nelly tightened her grip on Darlene's hand and cried out to her, "I'm afraid, let's go back!" "Don't be silly. This will be a once in a lifetime event," responded her friend. As they got closer, she heard the nervousness in the whinnying of the police horses.

The crowd chanted in unison, except this time they were calling the police names similar to swine and requesting that they breed with their mothers. They were demanding that the police leave the premises so they could occupy City Hall and force an immediate repeal of SB1070; anything short of that would be unacceptable.

With bullhorns blaring and fists pumping the air, the crowd continued onward despite the threats of tear gas from the Phoenix Police Department. Nelly heard a loud crack. She looked over and saw a young college student grabbing his face, blood gushing out of his nose; a tear gas cartridge had hit him in the face, and he went down.

The crowd went mad and turned into an angry mob. It was complete mayhem. The riot police started a parade of batons; they left screaming college students on the ground. They didn't walk on the grassroots, they stomped on them.

Nelly lost her friend and started to scream. She reached out blindly, in a cloud of gas. Her eyes burning, she couldn't see and quickly fell to the ground. She felt the weight of horse hooves trampling about her. People were stepping on her head, but she managed to get up. She staggered out, unfortunately, straight into the line of police, who quickly and with a swift blow to her face knocked her unconscious and threw her into a waiting paddy wagon.

She awoke in a blurred dream and saw a nurse in white. She couldn't talk, and then she went back into unconsciousness. When she eventually woke up, she found herself in a cell along with other women, some of whom she recognized from the rally. It was all coming back to her. She started asking for a police officer and began apologizing for anything she had done wrong. She promised that she would pay whatever fine was required, whatever it took.

The women in her cell began to laugh among themselves. One of the women she recognized from the rally came and sat next to her. As she stared at Nelly's badly broken nose and black eye, she said, "You're not in the police station, sweetie; you're in the immigration holding tank. As soon as your family gets here with your legal documents, they will let you go." Nelly's heart dropped to her stomach, she got sick, she felt nauseated, her whole body began to reject the moment; she barfed all over the place.

She was allowed to make a series of phone calls, so she called her friends. They arrived and pleaded with the clerks to release Nelly. They were finally allowed communication with Nelly, and they were surprised to find out her secret – Nelly was undocumented. They began to cry for each other in disbelief. How could this be? Darlene began apologizing for getting her into the mess. She promised that she would contact her cousin, Marty Silvers, a prominent attorney who'd known Nelly as a kid, when he was a freshman in college; a friend of the family.

The next day, Marty waited at the mayor's office. A secretary came into the waiting room, stood by the open office door, and said, "The mayor will see you now, Mr. Silvers." She made a motion with her right hand, not unlike a matador. "Come right on in."

Upon seeing Marty, the mayor got up out of his chair, extended his right hand to Marty and said, "What the F. Scott Fitzgerald?" "Great Gatsby!" answered Marty as they shook hands and laughed for a minute.

Marty knew Mel from his days as a public defender. Mel had been a prosecutor in the District Attorney's Office, and it wasn't uncommon for them to battle each other in the courtroom from time to time. They had mutual respect.

Then the conversation took a serious tone. "How are you, Martin? It's good to see you. However, I have to be up front with you on this one: No way! I'm getting a direct order straight from the top, from the Governor's Office; an example must be made. This cannot happen, we cannot allow a bunch of hippie socialist wetbacks to disrupt the flow of commerce!" stated the mayor.

"She's a goddamn prodigy, Mel! She is a decent, law-abiding citizen. Hell, she may be a candidate for a Harvard Law scholarship!" quipped Marty, frustrated.

"Oh yeah? What proof of citizenship will she show? Tell me. Huh, Marty? How in the hell are we going to give a scholarship to attend the finest American university to a damned wetback instead of our own?" replied the mayor. "Do you know how that would look, if it leaked into the media that we are promoting wetback high school students before our own? I would lose all my backers; this is not California!" he continued.

Marty gave the mayor an ultimatum. "Talk to the governor, INS, CPB, the DA, I don't care, convince them that she's good for us, or else I will go to the media. I will create the most bleeding-heart public relations event you ever imagined. I will put her in the spotlight, and we will block the entrance into Mexico and block your deportation at Nogales!" Marty stormed out of the office clutching his briefcase and mumbling legal jargon.

True to his word, Marty created a media frenzy. He invited all the media outlets, and they responded. CNN, Fox, the Associated Press, hell, even Matt Grudge showed up. Everyone had an opinion on the undocumented scholastic overachiever. Bill Reilly had a field day with her; he cut her up into little pieces, and the rest of the right wing media outlets were shredding her like a lawnmower on turbo.

The community, however, rallied behind her. She was now the poster child for the repeal of SB1070. "If we are deporting this future star, how many more have fallen through the cracks? We have already invested many years and resources; why not finish the investment so that they can become upstanding members of our community? This is America, the land of the free, not the land of the persecuted!" a community leader stated as he stood on a makeshift podium. He had the crowd in an uproar.

The community vowed to defend her by physical force if necessary; they were going to block the port of entry, or in this case the port of exit, at Nogales, Arizona. Thousands of people began gathering at the Nogales border into Mexico. They were chanting, they had picket signs and candlelight vigils; Nelly was their saint.

When the word got out, thousands more began gathering at additional ports of entry into Sonora, Mexico. Towards the east they gathered at the ports of entry at Naco, which entered into Naco, Sonora, Mexico, and at Douglas, which entered into Agua Prieta. Towards the west they gathered at Sasabe, which entered into Altar, and further west yet, at the Lukeville and San Luis ports, which entered into Sonoita and San Luis Rio Colorado.

In a government building filled with immigration officers, city attorneys, and business leaders, men in suits gathered to strategize on the best way to avoid a public relations fiasco. A low voice spoke into the telephone: "The decision has been made. Deport her through the San Ysidro Port of Entry, San Diego, California, today!" "That's an eight hour drive, Sir," responded the voice on the other end.

Click, the phone went dead.

A Journey to San Diego

It was cramped in the Border Patrol van built for eight but carrying twelve. Half of them spoke fluent English. It was one hundred and one degrees in the Arizona morning. Beads of sweat poured from the brows of the illegals cramped up in the back. Dehydrated,

demoralized and mostly forgotten, they took their grief like a badge of honor. Nelly sat quietly among a ragtag assortment of people she normally would never have socialized with. She didn't even speak Spanish. They were from all over the place and from different walks of society.

Most wore the clothes they were caught in: work clothes, leisure wear or party duds, guys wore faded tees emblazoned with Abercrombie & Fitch, Aeropostale, Hollister or whatever knockoffs they'd bought at the swap meet, the women wore jeans, or leggings, or, in Nelly's case, pink short shorts and a pink belly shirt with matching high tops. A tough tattooed gang member wore an Oakland Raiders Jersey.

Nelly sat next to a quiet, polite-looking young man. His fingernails looked dirty but trimmed, his fingers dainty. His name was Luis; he was soft-spoken. She knew he would not try to get fresh or try anything on her on the eight-hour drive to California. Across from her was a menacing thug with a tattooed face and neck. He looked like he was crying because he had a teardrop on his eye – or maybe that was also a tattoo. He was staring out the window towards the horizon.

"Okay, sons of bitches, you all settled in? Yee haw! Let's go for a ride," shouted Jack, one of two Border Patrol officers charged with escorting the cargo of undocumented people. He banged on all the outside windows, startling the men and women inside who would have otherwise settled in for the long drive. Nelly sensed that this man would be a problem.

"Come on, Jack, give 'em a break. Give *me* a break, for heaven's sake. We are just starting this here shit drive." Sergeant Rob, the driver and officer in charge, was a mellow middle-aged man with an easy disposition. He could be tough when warranted, but otherwise just left everyone alone.

He went to talk to the people in the back of the van. "We're going to make three stops, *comprende?*" They all nodded as if they understood, but only half of them spoke English. "Two bathroom and water stops, with a lunch break in between at the four-hour mark." He spoke in a loud voice, as if a louder voice would help them understand. "Yeah, they don't understand a damn thing I'm saying," he grumbled under his breath as he peered into the van windows to make sure everything was fine.

He had a case of water bottles and handed each person two bottles, which they eagerly grabbed. Nelly pleaded with the officer. She told him that this was all a mistake, that she didn't belong in the van; she spoke perfect English, and tried to convince the officer to let her make one last phone call. He explained that as much as he would like to help her, he had his orders and that he always followed his orders. He told Nelly that once she got to Tijuana she could make phone calls and notify the proper authorities.

As he finished talking she whispered to the officer, "Please, please, you have to help me, I don't belong here, I don't belong here, please, officer!"

The English speakers mimicked her in an unflattering voice: "Please, please, I'm so special officer, I was framed!... Ha, ha!" They laughed, and still others yelled out, "I'll do anything you want, mister, come on, me love you long time! Ha!" They were having a good time at Nelly's expense. Officer Rob then got into the driver's seat, put a tape in the van's cassette player – The Eagles, "Hotel California," an appropriate tune – turned the ignition key, and drove them on their way.

"Hey, amigo, you want to change places with me, huh? She's too much for you, huh?" The semi-whisper came from Pretty Boy. It was directed toward Luis. Pretty Boy had his eye on Nelly, who had seen better days, still wearing the bloodied pink belly shirt and pink Converse All Stars Chuck Taylors, her normally impeccable hair all frayed. She was trying to avoid any conversation with these people and trying to make the trip without getting raped. She clutched Luis's jacket arm and whispered a commanding, "Don't you freegin' move!" Pretty Boy sat next to Psyko and directly across from Luis.

Pretty Boy and Psyko were immediately drawn to each other because of their tough backgrounds, an honor among thieves type thing, or maybe these types just found each other in crowds. Sitting to the left of Pretty Boy was Reymundo, a 50-year-old ex-preacher, a big, affable old guy; he had a way with words. Next to Reymundo was Don Felipe, a small old guy who was trying to sleep off a hangover. He had been busted that morning, by chance, when a passing Border Patrol vehicle almost ran him over. He'd been sleeping in the middle of the road after an all-night bender.

Next to Luis, on the other side, was Doña Rosa, a housekeeper. A short, round lady with skinny legs and a strong back, she was normally the nicest person you could meet but in these circumstances, she was withdrawn. Her cheeks were red and raw from wiping away so many tears. All she could think of was her babies. Did they get home safely? Did her husband realize that she was being deported? What was to become of them? What was to become of her?

Next to Doña Rosa was a young, smiling 19-year-old, Orelio "Yeyo" Esparza, from Central America. He really had no idea what was going on, just that he was being deported; he'd bounced around the systems here and there as much as he bounced on that seat from the bumpy ride. He'd been arrested in Nebraska and waited in an immigration detention center for two weeks before being moved around and eventually ending up in Arizona. Yeyo was truly invisible; nobody would ever notice if he went missing. A young vagabond of sorts; he'd taken the death train to El Norte as if it were a bus ride on a Sunday afternoon.

The van benches were arranged one bench on each side, facing each other. Six people per bench on a bench built for four. The sound of the van engine starting made everyone begin to ease into their seats, and then the van began to roll forward. "*Oye, amigo*, I got some killer bud. Here, smell my finger!" Pretty Boy cackled as his head bobbed around, entertaining himself.

The musty smell of musk, skunk and sweat was unbearable. Nelly wanted to puke but was too tired. Pretty Boy made a motion with his hand, as if to touch her, to test Nelly. "Get your filthy damned hands off me," she growled in her deepest, most menacing voice. She was dying inside.

"*Calmate pinche Bandera Americana!*" he answered her.
"*Por que le dices asi?*" said Luis. *Why you call her like that?*
"*Por que a esa, se la han clavado hasta en la luna!*"
She pretended not to understand, but although Nelly didn't speak fluent Spanish she understood bits and pieces. He had called her "American Flag" because she had been penetrated even on the moon – he was saying she was promiscuous.

Nelly could not stop thinking of her life. How did this all happen? Why her? All her life she was the perfect daughter, the perfect student. She always got A's in both academics as well as citizenship. She was a volunteer and a model student. Why had her perfect life come crumbling down?

"Man, Pretty Boy, leave that skank bitch alone, can't you see some *vato* already gave her a black eye and busted up her shit? She thinks she's too good for you but she ain't nothing but a *mojada*." A wetback.

Nelly tried hard to keep that tear from rolling down her cheek. But her eyes welled up and the big, fat tear rolled down, stopping at the blood that stained her halfway down her cheek and rerouting towards the back of her neck. She slowly turned away so they could not see her weakness. Luis gave her a reassuring, warm grip on her back, as soft as she would receive from any her BFFs back home; she felt better.

"What's your name?" she whispered to him. "Luis Anselmo Rivera, I am a horse trainer; ever since I was a boy I was good with horses. I lived on a large ranch in Carolina del Sur," he replied in a soothing, almost hypnotic tone.

"Horse trainer? What are you, in the circus?" she asked.
"No, I groom, clean, brush the horses in my patron's stables, and once a day we take turns with each horse, preparing…"
Luis was rudely interrupted by Psyko. "You take turns on the horse, you sick son of a bitch? You are a freegin *puto maricon* huh? I knew it, all soft and shit?"

"Shut the hell up, stupid *Cholo*! Just because a man has manners, is polite and not rude, he has to be automatically gay, right? You're a stupid homophobe!" Nelly was feeling a sense of courage, like when a wild animal is cornered and has to either fight or flee. However, she had no place to flee; all she had was fight, and fight she did.

"A homo what!" responded an angry Psyko, putting emphasis on the T in his enunciation. "A homophobe. You fear what you don't know. You think you are going to go gay if you come in contact with a homosexual because you yourself are unsure about your manhood." She turned to Luis, held his hand and said, "I'm not saying you're a homosexual, Luis, I'm just saying if you are, that's fine and nobody should persecute you. Especially some lowlife wannabe gang banger who needs to stay out of our conversation," she said as she glared back at Psyko.

"Whatever, crazy *mojada bandera Americana*," said Psyko as he turned and rolled his eyes, no longer amused with the conversation.

The *mojada* comment cut Nelly deeply, but she refrained from showing emotions.

"Man, she done mess your shit up, Cholo, what the hell, man, you a hard mutha-effer and you're gonna let some prom queen shut you up?" Pretty Boy turned his attention to Luis and asked a series of questions.

Pretty Boy: "Okay, let me get this straight, *hombre rana*. You wash and clean the horses?
Luis: "Yes."
Pretty Boy: "The hoofs and shit?"
Luis: "Yes."
Pretty Boy: "The tail? The butthole?"
Psyko laughed.
Luis: "No, not there, of course not!"
Pretty Boy: "His dick?"
Luis: "Of course his you-know-what, horses can develop melanomas. You have to clean the sheath from the... you know...."
Pretty Boy: "Dick! Hold on, wait, wait, wait. Hold on a minute, you mean to tell me you grab the horse's dick?"
Luis, annoyed: "Yes!"
Pretty Boy: "In your hand and then you clean it with the other?"
Luis, upset: "YES!"
Pretty Boy, looking at Luis in disgust: "You horse cock-stroking son of a bitch, you must love your job!"
Pretty Boy made a jacking-off gesture with his hand, then pounded fists with a laughing Psyko and mumbled under his breath, "*Pinche homo, pinche hombre rana.*"

Psyko had to ask, "Why you call him *hombre rana?*"
Pretty Boy responded, loud and laughing, "*Por que si le sacan el tubo se muere!*" The whole van erupted in laughter, even Luis cracked up at that one, while Nelly shook her head, pretending she was insulted but holding her laughter.

Pretty Boy kept referring to Luis as *hombre rana* – frogman, a snorkeler – because he couldn't live without a tube inside him; a reference to his effeminate mannerisms. Reymundo, still laughing, chastised the young guns, ending their spree of one-liners.

Reymundo began telling the people around him about his Aztec research and how they should all be proud of their roots. "Let me tell you the story of your people," started Reymundo.

"Not my people, I'm an American!" replied Nelly.
"Yeah, we can see you're an American, because they deport Americans every day!" Pretty Boy responded while he and Psyko laughed.

Reymundo defended her. "That's okay. Many Americans have deep roots in the Aztec culture. If you guys don't have anything better to do, I can tell you guys some stories about where the Azteca Nation, the People of the Sun, come from. My people, your people, Yeyo's people." He began speaking in a voice that came from within his soul.

The Rise and Fall of Aztatlan – In the Beginning

In the beginning, there was a land, a land in paradise. In this land
lived a people, the people of the Sun God. The Sun God chose these
people that they would rule the land for the Sun God; he was pleased
with the people. One thousand years they lived and prospered in this
land, a land located in the north part of the Western Hemisphere, in
the west side of the continent, by the sea; the land of Aztatlan.

They were successful warriors, hunters, farmers. Their civilization
was very advanced for the time. Aztatlan was the envy of all other
peoples who lived in the south and east and north. They were truly
the chosen people. The Sun God provided the Aztatlanteans victories
in war, in the hunt, in agriculture; the people of the Sun God
multiplied, and the Sun God was pleased.

This was in the time when jaguars roamed and ruled the northern
continent. The tribes were not safe because rogue cats haunted the
nights, entering the tribal compounds and running off with the weak,
the young or the sick. Patrols were set up around the perimeter on the
lookout for the dangerous beasts.

As the civilization grew, its descendants became corrupted by the
wealth and power of their success. They claimed their place with the
Sun God as equals. They used their sacred knowledge to conquer
other tribes of people. The Sun God became displeased, angry.

The Sun God came down in the form of a man. He dressed in
beautiful blue, green and white feathers; he had the face of the stars,
the strength of the jaguar and the cleverness of the *coyotl*, or coyote.
He came down to save his chosen people from destruction.

Now Ixtzoc was a good Aztatlantean, a direct descendant of Tzacol,
one of the original people who came from below the *tlalli*, or earth.
The earth was the most valuable resource in the Universe, created by
the Sun God; it was valued for its ability to be molded into anything,

even man. So in the beginning, the Sun God had created the seven men of clay from below the earth, the Chicomoztoc.

Now Ixtzoc had just finished his daily toil, his labor; his lands were rich and his people were plenty. He drank of the sacred *atole,* a mixture of cornmeal, *chocotl,* alcohol, and peppers; he fell into a deep sleep. "Ixtzoc!" the Sun God called unto him. "Ixtzoc!" called the mighty deity, but Ixtzoc did not respond, because he was in a slumber. "Ixtzoc!" called the Sun God a third time. The man awoke frightened and still in a daze. "I am here. I am afraid, Lord, because I did not prevent the people of Aztatlan, your people, from becoming corrupt, and I am to blame." Ixtzoc began to weep.

The Sun God took pity on Ixtzoc and said unto him, "Ixtzoc, you are my son and I will guide you and your descendants away from this land, which has become corrupt and wicked. I will bring the four waters, the Nahuatl, and there will be a destruction like never seen before."

Ixtzoc was afraid but had faith in the Sun God who had nurtured his people from the beginning. Ixtzoc asked, "Where will we go? There is a body of water to the west, and the tribes of the east and the north will surely vanquish me and my people."

The Sun God directed Ixtzoc to go south, toward the southeast, specifically, toward the people of the land of Anahuac. Ixtzoc knew the people of that land. They were fierce and even more savage and primitive than the people of the east or the north; Ixtzoc began to weep again.

The Sun God spoke. "Calm yourself, I will make your sons the greatest warriors the world has ever seen; I will inspire them to fight on, they will conquer the people of Anahuac. You will build my temples and sacrifice a great many *yaotl,* or warriors. We will seal the great covenant, and you will ensure that I rise from the east every day with your sacrifices. The stars and the sun will forever be in constant battle. You will sacrifice for me, as I have sacrificed for you."

Reymundo went back to his regular voice and said to them, "So that is why you young *vatos* need to leave these two alone. We're all in this together. We still have a long way to go, isn't it better if we all get along?" Reymundo was sitting next to Pretty Boy. He had heard the entire conversation, but had held his tongue until now.

Doña Rosa and Yeyo were having their own conversation in Spanish, as were the rest of the passengers. Reymundo wore an old blue baseball hat; it must have been 10 years old. He was a beast of a man with a gentle but twisted soul. Always trying to make the peace between opposing forces and always leaving himself for last, confident that his own needs would surely be met in time.

Nicknames-*Apodos*

Mexicans have an infatuation with *apodos,* or nicknames. They just can't leave well enough alone. Part of it is that natural tendency that each of us has to adapt or arrange everything in our lives according to our needs. When we get a new vehicle, we add the fancy wheels and the ear-busting stereo, or a favorite sports team sticker on the back window. When we get into a new sleeping quarter, we arrange it first, so that we feel our feng shui will best be served, even if we don't have the slightest idea what feng shui is. "Yeah, uh, waiter? Um, could you give me some Kung Pao chicken with a side of extra crispy feng shui?"

The other reason we change people's names is camaraderie. We want the people in our lives to be our own. Yeah, the world may know you by a certain, given name, but we will christen you with a new one. Maybe it will be a short version of your name or maybe something that reflects your appearance – often it's unexplainable. Consider some examples of this phenomenon. You meet up with some new friends for a weekend in the country; they ask you your name and then reply by calling you a different name.

"Hello, what's your name?" they ask.
"My name is Alicia," you respond.
"*Hola*, Licha!" they say. "I am Concepcion, but you can call me Conchita. This is my good friend Euralia, but you can call her Lala."
"I can't call her by her real name?" you ask naively.
"That is her real name," they assure you.
"Over there, that is Dolores. You can call her Lolita. And that *cabrona* over there, that's Rosario, you can call her slut! Just kidding, we call her Chayo. We're going to go pick up maca," they say.

Of course you say, "Let me guess, that's short for Macaria, right?"
"No," they respond with a bewildered look, like what you said is so crazy it's beyond comprehension; it's out of this world. "What are you talking about? No, *hamacha* (pronounced a-maw-cah)," they

quip. "You know, a hammock, you ever slept on a hammock, a *hamacha*? We're picking up *hamachas* for the camping trip; you want to sleep comfortable, right?" they continue. "Oh, okay, whatever. Excuse me!" is all you can come up with.

If you're the fairer skinned of any group, you automatically get tagged as Guero or Guera (blonde), and if you're fair skinned and a good-looking girl you are Guerita (Blondie). Americans get the Guero nickname a lot because they're fairer in skin color than most Mexicans. Sometimes Mexicans will add creative adornment to words when describing a white guy, especially if the white guy is a cop who just gave them a ticket and thus becomes "*Pinche Guero Puto!*" Nice.

Inversely, if you're the darkest of the group you have the honor of being El Indio or Negro. Now, it is not pronounced Negro, as in the baseball Negro League, no sir, it's pronounced like you're saying "neck-grow," you know?
Example:

"Doctor, I know I shouldn't have been playing the part of the bull, ramming the wall and smashing my head into my torso. Now I look like I'm always shrugging my shoulders to say 'I don't know,' but Doctor, if I keep going through therapy, will my neck grow?"

If you give off a Far Eastern or Asian look, you are automatically christened China (pronounced Cheena) or Chino (Cheeno).
If you enjoy the fruit of the vine more than your comrades (you're a drunk), you become El Chupes (one who sucks), because you "suck" from the bottle, or *chupas la botella*. "Hey, meester, your jokes really *chupes*!" Yeah, I know, thanks.

One memorable name that always seems to get chosen for the most ragtag of the bunch is Cero (pronounced Seto), which sounds like the translation of zero in Spanish. You'd think that would sound exotic, even cool. "Hey, there goes Cero cold as ice, man. What a cool dude, he's got the coolest name in town. He must get all the girls." But that's not what they mean.

Cero is short for Cerote (Seto-tay), which means turd in Spanish. Picture yourself in a club. "Hey ladies, my name is Cero. Yeah, let me give you my business card." Now imagine your friends C-blocking you from afar. "Hey, Cerote, come over here, leave those girls alone!" The ladies move away, grossed out. "Ew, gross. Get away from me, Turd Boy." This moniker is reserved only for the most deserving friends, with a good sense of humor.

Then of course there are the standard, run-of-the-mill nicknames like Gordo (Fatso) if all your friends weigh less than you. "Hey, Gordo, come over here. I want to introduce you to a buddy of mine. Holy cow! My new buddy is fatter than you. Okay, you are no longer Gordo, he's Gordo, and you could be Gordo Light or One Calorie Gordo. Gordo Zero?"

El Bigotes (Stash) if you have the biggest mustache of the gang, El Pecas (Freckles) for the freckle-faced buddy, Afro for the guy with the big curly hair, and Morro (Youngin') for the youngest of the crew. Sometimes Mocoso (Snots) works well for the younger ones as well.

Then, of course, you have standard shortened versions of your Christian name. For example: Chuey, which is short for Jesus (Hey-Zeus).
Imagine the following scenario:

Mom: "Hey, honey, your little Hispanic friend is here to see you. I forgot his name, I thinks it's Crunchy or something like that; here, have some homemade brownies."
You (grabbing a brownie and taking a bite): "Chuey."
Mom: "Well, yeah, they're brownies. They're supposed to be kind of chewy, silly."
You: "No, Mom, his name is Chuey."

Chema for Jose Maria, and Lalo for Eduardo, now that sounds cool as hell. "There goes Lalo cruising in his Lolo, yeah boy! Westside!

Lupita replaces Guadalupe. I worked with a girl named Guadalupe; we called her Lupe for short. Being the efficient workforce that we were, we shortened it to the one-syllable name, Loops. Of course, we eventually came full circle and began using the clever Fruit Loops. Wouldn't you know, we wound up calling her Kellogg's. The last time I called and asked for her at her work, a guy answered the phone, and when I asked for Guadalupe, he put the phone down and yelled "Kelly, it's for you!"

Mila for Emilia, which, like Lalo, sounds like some cool movie star name. Nacho for Ignacio; Iggy works here as well, and Pepe for Jose. Now that one, nobody can explain. I could understand Che for Jose, which works out well, but Pepe? The explanation for that was lost with the map to the Aztec gold.

Loly is short for Gloria, which sounds like a happy name, right? But it's pronounced "lowly." When you say it, it sounds like you're saying "lonely." So Loly may be mistaken for a person who has no companions. Which leads me to another potential scenario:

You: "Yo, dawg, I want to introduce you to my sister. This here is Loly."
Your friend: "What's up, girl? Why you so sad? I'll be your friend, you'll never be lonely again!"
Keep it in your pants, dawg.

Toño for Antonio, and Kiki for Enrique. For Francisco, which actually sounds very feminine because of the Francis part at the front, we have the Triple Crown of nicknames; this bad boy gets either Chico, Paco or Pancho. All very cool names in their own right; choose wisely.

For Guillermo, I can offer you Memo with a Willie to be named later. As with Pepe, there are no known texts in the ancient archives explaining how Guillermo becomes William – it doesn't exist, so don't ask.

Tavo for Gustavo, you've got to admit that nickname, like Mila, sounds cool, like a male model; maybe the name of new cologne, "Tavo by Hugo Boss."

Lencho for Lorenzo, Momo for Jeronimo. Momo, hell yeah! Which leads me to yet another scenario:

Shady character: "Wassup, Momo, where you been? Everybody been looking for you man, the whole gang, you know? Jimmy da Cheese, Joey Bag-O-Donuts, Boom-Boom Belinda, they all wanna know where you been, man."
Momo: "Fuhget about it!"

For George or Jorge there is Coky, Rafa for Rafael, Chava for Salvador, and of course there is my favorite, Chalino for Rosalino. Somebody better open up a bottle of Patron and put on some "Nieves de Enero" by Chalino Sanchez, so we can all have a good cry; yes, we're drinking tonight!

I guess this is not limited to Mexican folk or even Latinos. Americans, Canadians, Europeans, and – I'm not sure about this one – I think even the Chinese are guilty of a little name changing and nicknaming. It's our way of personalizing our friends, I suppose.

Horse Trainer – *El Ranas*

The sound of strumming from a guitar, accompanied by the twang of Don Bob's banjo, created a musical background to the picturesque scene – a lazy evening outdoor mini concerto.

"La da dum, la da di, pum pum pum pum, la da da.

Take my tired soul, hasta la vista, porque ya te termine de amar
Pues que no ves que me rechazan, y solamente lagrimas secas
quedaron

Take my empty, empty heart, cause there's nothing left to give,
I've loved you well as good as him, but unlike him, I've gone away.

La da dum, la da di, pum pum pum pum, la da di, la da da. da di.

If you ever you could see my loneliness, today would be the time,
Our souls, they dance apart like lovers blind.

Take my battered heart, hasta la vista,
My empty heart can sing no more..."

Luis sang the most beautiful Spanglish lyrics off the top of his head with his patron Don Bob (pronounced Dough'n Bob) on banjo, after the work was done on that South Carolina horse ranch overlooking the Atlantic Ocean. Green pastures as far as the eye could see and silhouettes of beautiful horses galloping and playing in the early dusk as the sun went down. Luis was a hopeless romantic who was good with horses but better at songwriting and playing classical guitar.

Don Bob was a descendant of Civil War heroes; he kept a Confederate soldier's uniform his great great grandpappy had worn in battle. He proudly displayed an 1863 cannon ball on his fireplace mantle, a memento compliments of an advancing Union army unit's cannon fire that shot through his great great grandpappy's kitchen before they were repelled by the local chapter of the Confederate Soldiers of Seceded America.

Don Bob's great great grandpappy, Addison Montrose Hickman, had kept the cannon ball on his fireplace mantle as a reminder of that frightful day. He'd passed it on to his son Tobias Jefferson Hickman, who'd passed it on to his son Jasper Addison Hickman, who'd passed it on to Don Bob's father, Robert Montrose Hickman, who, in turn, passed it on to his son Robert Delford Hickman, also known Bob, or as Luis called him, Don Bob or Mr. Bob; a sign of respect.

He would sing songs with Luis and then drink bourbon, though Luis wasn't much of a drinker, mostly choking and gagging on the strong drink. He would one minute start hugging Luis, professing his eternal friendship and saying he would treat him like a son, then another minute he would abruptly cry out, "You see that cannon ball sittin baw the fawplace, boy?"

"Yes, the bowling ball, correct?" Luis would reply.
 "Ain't no goddam bowlin bawl, boy!!!" He stumbled towards Luis as he swung his cane at Luis's head; Luis ducked, anticipating the old man's walking stick or *malacca*, as Luis usually called it.

Although he was a good and just man, he was a mean drunk; this ritual would replay itself every night. Luis was too afraid to leave the secure compound, and Don Bob had chased away any remnant of a friend and only had his trusty worker Luis to tend to his horses and keep him company. They only had each other, except, of course, for Black Pete Kimbo, a blind octogenarian who had a 20-year-old granddaughter, Marie, a beautiful half-white, half-black *mulata*.

They would visit from time to time to play harmonica and banjo, sing and dance, until Don Bob would get drunk and re-enact Civil War battles. Everyone knew at that point the party was over.

A sweet smell of fresh jasmine filled the autumn air. The ranch was enchanting but was also a house of torment, a golden cage for Luis, an effeminate young man with dreamy eyes. His delicate ways created harmony with the horses, who would scare easily if he were not around. All his life Luis was taunted with the same hateful word that had followed him to America from his own father's ranch in Matamoros. *Puto, puto, puto*, the word haunted him every night, so much that he'd rarely made friends growing up.

His mother would defend him from daily beatings from his father, who saw him as a curse from God. His only son was a *puto*, a *maricon* (gay), so what if he was amazing with horses? He'd wanted a son who was a bronco buster, not a brokeback soft girly lady that ran to his momma's skirt every time he sensed danger, which was often growing up in macho Mexico.

Along a picturesque pasture beneath the South Carolina sky, with an ocean backdrop, Luis and Marie rode two beautiful horses along an untouched, serene area too perfect to believe, truly heaven on earth. They pointed out the natural wonders, the birds and the trees with leaves rustling in the gentle breeze; they rode for what seemed like hours and stopped at their favorite spot.

They got off the horses and set a picnic spread. She set out a checkerboard tablecloth. Marie had made lunch for them: yard bird, salad and cornbread, with a bottle of wine from her grampy's stash. She always said that he shouldn't be drinking too much anyway, because he'd forget to take his medicine and it would upset his stomach, and she had to search the premises to find him usually passed out in the chicken coop or by the pig pen.

After they dined, they looked out at the ocean. The day was perfect, the day was winding down, and Luis suggested, "Let's dance?" Marie immediately jumped up, because she knew what that meant.

He looked her in the eyes and softly sang "Last Dance" by Donna Summer, one of his favorite tunes from when he was a boy in Mexico. His aunt had brought an old 78 record from her trip to America back when it had first come out; he wasn't even born then.

He held Marie's hand, a romantic gaze as his eyes met hers. She was in love with him, but realized that their love would never be, so she consoled herself, knowing that she had a friend for life. He sang the tune while dancing. A tear rolled down her face, and he continued to sing the song. She smiled a big smile because of what would follow. He swung her around, and they began a perfect dance worthy of an invitation to audition for Soul Train.

He twirled her; she responded, and they were in perfect sync. He continued to sing, his vibrato echoing in the air, the horses excited as if to join in, as birds flew above the courtship dance. They separated and began a series of silly dance moves in perfect rhythm, standing side by side; they did a Disco Duck, flapping their arms while shuffling their feet. They morphed into a crazy C-Walk, then Luis did a little old-school pop-lock – Marie cracked up every time he did that – then the Robot, which always took center stage, the riding horsey, the running man, and the Melbourne Shuffle. They always ended with Luis holding Marie in a long, lowered pose as though they were ending a fancy Tango. She straightened up; they'd played this out a million times, and a million times they'd nailed it.

The beauty of the day was short lived. As they rode back, they came across a couple of rednecks. They didn't look at the men, but the two old boys were hard mad-dogging them, spewing out ugly epithets; "Look at what we got here, a taco and a chitlin." They cracked up, and Luis and Marie ignored them. The men, seeing that they couldn't get through, went about their business. Luis looked at Marie and said, "Chitlin?"

She laughed and said, "Come on, let's go, Taco."
He responded "*Prrrrrrrr, aye, aye, aye, andale, andale, andale!*" and they both rode off in laughter.
Marie had something on her mind but didn't know how to relay it. She finally interrupted Luis, who was telling her about his recipe for Frijoles Charro. "Luis, I need to tell you something."
"Yes?" he replied.

"It's actually wonderful news, but is also bad news."
"What is it, *amiga*? Tell me now, you have me worried."
"Well, the good news is I've been accepted into University of South Carolina, I'm going to be a gamecock!"
"*Felicidades!*" replied Luis.

"Thanks, but the bad news is I have to go away. I have been postponing this, but soon I will be going," responded Marie. He was sad but happy for his best friend at the same time. They hugged and he assured her that he was fine. His soul had just been split in two. She knew that without her, he would be vulnerable to the wolves of the world.

As time passed, Marie went off to college; old Pete and Luis drove her to the bus station. They said their goodbyes, and she promised to return on Christmas break. The bus drove off; old Pete waved as if he could see it go, but he was waving in the wrong direction. Luis, who was locked elbow to elbow with the old man, gently corrected the direction of his wave about 90 degrees.

Luis continued to take care of the horses on the ranch. On one particular cold day, before Thanksgiving, the skies were dark; he sensed that the horses were upset.

When he finished, he went to Don Bob's main house to report the state of business. As he stepped into the den, he found Don Bob dressed in the Civil War uniform, pistol to his head. Luis's eyes opened wide, and before he could say a word, Don Bob pulled the trigger and fell to the floor. Luis, in horror, ran to him, but it was too late, about one third of his head was missing from the other side; blood was everywhere. Luis began to cry while holding his old friend and boss. Next to Don Bob was a letter from a financial institution, a foreclosure notice. His family ranch was being foreclosed for failure to pay.

The next day Don Bob's estranged son arrived to arrange for a funeral and close his father's pending business transactions. He needed to remove items that he had inherited; antiques, anything that he could keep to remind him of his family's past. He talked to Luis, told him that he and his father had not spoken in twenty years. He also told Luis that he would need to find another place to live because the bank had foreclosed on the house and all of the horses. He gave Luis twenty-four hours to leave the premises. He apologized to him, thanked him for being a friend to his father, but told him that this was business; it was not up to him. He gave Luis two twenty dollars bills; he suggested that Luis return to Mexico. Luis, never anticipating such a short-notice eviction, had been sending the majority of his weekly salary to his mother in Mexico. He was broke and had no place to go.

Luis had few acquaintances; he had spent the last fifteen years on this property, and rarely ventured out to the big cities. He was afraid but had a strong determination to get ahead and back into the saddle, so to speak. He went to old Pete's house to say goodbye. The old man told him he was going to miss him and that he would tell Marie. "Send a postcard when you get to where you're gonna go so Marie can write to you." They hugged. Luis tightened his grip on the old man as tears rolled down his eyes, but the old man could not see that Luis was crying. "Yawl take care now," Pete told him as Luis went on his way with only a water bottle and a backpack full of memories.

Luis was walking down a lonely Dixie highway, hitchhiking his way to California (the song "For the Dreamers" by Myriad 3 played on his headphones); he'd heard that there were many horse ranches and Hispanics there. The sky was grey and gloomy. Despite the headphones he could hear the sound of an approaching car. He put his thumb out; he'd been walking for seven hours. A set of headlights could be seen behind him as Luis was singing tunes; the vehicle came closer, and Luis quickly and excitedly turned around. Then Luis noticed that it was an immigration van.

Luis darted down the shoulder of the road into the landscape, which was full of trees and brush. An officer chased him. Luis was still wearing his headphones; he was trying to run at full speed but he felt himself running in slow motion, as in a dream. He stumbled and rolled down an embankment. The officer beat him for running; a bloodied and zip-tied Luis was loaded into the van.

On the side of the road Luis's backpack lay alone in the dirt. An officer picked it up, opened the side door and threw it at Luis, who was in and out of consciousness. He thought about the time when he'd crossed into America; the rain began to pour down. Luis was taken to a detention facility in Texas, where he was held for six months.

Reymundo noticed the people were all in a depressed state, and being the man that he was, he continued the story he had started earlier. "So let me continue this story about our ancestors." Everyone around him sat up, encouraged. Even Nelly paid attention.

The Rise and Fall of Aztatlan II – The Exodus

Now Ixtzoc gathered his people and told them about the vision that the Sun God had given him in his sleep. The people of Ixtzoc respected him greatly, so they gathered all their belongings and fled the land in a caravan of mass migration to the southeast, to the land of Anahuac. As they left their homeland they came across a great plain, an elevated mountain plateau. They made camp for the period of a moon and a star.

There was a great deluge as the four waters came from above, from below, from the great ocean to the west, and from air in the winds of the hurricanes; Nahuatl was upon the land of Aztatlan. Ixtzoc saw from a great distance perched safely atop his plateau; the skies were black and the waters from the Nahuatl had reached their mountain, which was now an island.

Ixtzoc instructed the people to build water vessels, *chalupas*, so as to travel away from the mountain towards their destination. The sons of Ixtzoc were noble men, fair and just, but the other nobility who came along were jealous of the power of the lineage of Ixtzoc, a humble man. One particular man who questioned the wisdom of Ixtzoc was Ixtli Cualli, or Good Face. He was called this because of his perfect features. Ixtli Cualli, a warrior, was a vain man who attained riches from the commoners because his attractive features made him a popular warrior.

Ixtli Cualli's thirst for power became apparent after the exodus and reared its ugly head once the people of the Sun of God were out of danger of the Nahuatl. Many *chalupas* were built from reeds and *hule* – rubber – and were set on the water for transport away from the island and back towards the migration route. Ixtli Cualli led the way. In all, the people of the Sun of God traveled for about two years. At the end of the first year, halfway through their voyage, they came across an oracle near a waterfall. It was the Sun God; he was dressed in white robes with a glowing face as bright as the sun. He gathered the leaders, including the sons of Ixtzoc and Ixtli Cualli.

The Sun God spoke: "I am the Sun God, but I am no longer the Sun God of Aztatlan. I have destroyed Aztatlan, for they were a wicked people. I chose the people of Ixtzoc, descendant of Tixzoc, who I made from the earth's bosom. From now on, there will be a new covenant. You will be known as the Mexitli, and your people will be the Mexica; you will know me as Huitzilopochtli, the Sun God." They made camp for a season in the wilderness.

They were instructed to burn all known sacred codices and belief systems. Huitzilopochtli instructed the Mexica in the ways in which to sacrifice and perform the new scared rituals to comply with the new covenant. Mexitli was a humble servant of Huitzilopochtli, but when he went to war he was as fierce as any of the young warriors. They needed to find sacrificial warriors; they traveled for six moons, and came across a southern tribe, which welcomed the Mexica; a tribe with no country.

Reymundo stopped his story, looking at the young man, the horse trainer, who had a new name, Ranas. He said, "What's the matter with you, *vato*, it looks like you've seen a ghost."
"No sir, it's just that the story reminded me of my own experience, the time I crossed illegally here to the United States. That was fifteen years ago. I barely spoke English, and it was not a pleasant time for me."

Reymundo felt that Luis had to get his story out so that he could release the hurt he held inside, even if Psyko and Pretty Boy injected degrading comments for their own amusement.

The Trek

Luis was walking in a procession in the Mexican mountains across
the U.S. border; there were about twelve guys and one young girl.
They were hiking up a mountainous area full of chaparral. They
looked towards the northern horizon; the sky was red, it was dusk.
They stopped as the lead guy gave instructions to them all to sit and
wait.

He told them in Spanish, with a finger outstretched toward the north,
"See that? That is America, we will be there in thirty hours. It won't
be easy and you will go through things and pains, frustrations you
never imagined, but I will get you there. Now, anyone who has any
doubt about whether they have the *huevos* to make it, turn around
through that path now. After this there will be no turning back. If you
listen to every word I tell you I promise you will not get caught. Stay
quiet, be fast, and save every drop of water you can. Is everyone
ready?" A collective "*Sí*" resounded through the quiet, hot, sweet
desert air.

Fernando, who everybody called Nano, was the coyote. He told them
that he would be in the middle of the line as they went and, if they
got caught somehow, nobody was to rat him out or they would be
killed along with their families. He looked at a dark young man and
told him in Spanish, "Morro, you will be my lead guy. You're quick
and sharp, don't worry, you'll be fine." The young man nodded his
head reluctantly. Luis was placed at the rear of the line with the
young girl and her brother.

A scary looking man with no soul in his eyes was in front of Luis,
they called him Demonio. Nano told the lead man, Morro, which
direction to go and when to slow, duck or stop. They hiked down the
last hill located on Mexican soil and began to climb the next
mountain, into the United States of America. Each one was carrying
only two three-quart plastic containers full of water; one was in each
hand as they struggled to carry the heavy bottles. Nano assured them

that pretty soon, they would be glad they carried them. Each one was also carrying a backpack with food and supplies.

The girl looked at her brother and told him something. "Shut up," Nano barked. The girl looked at Luis, embarrassed. Luis pretended not to notice she'd been chastised, and looked away. They marched on all through the night, through weaving trails, up and down hills and coves. Night crawling animals scurried away about their feet: snakes, lizards, but everyone was too tired to pay attention.

The pace was intense, a determined march. At about two in the morning Nano told them that they could take a two-hour nap but that they would be on their way after that, anyone who lagged would be stuck alone in the hot desert landscape. They hunkered down close to each other; it was cold and you could hear the distant cries of coyotes all night long. Nano assured them that as long as nobody separated from the pack they would not be eaten; he wasn't playing.

Luis awakened to the sound of rustling clothes. Demonio was straddling the girl while holding her mouth. He was whispering that if she made a sound he would slice her brother's neck and then hers; participate willingly or his cousin Nano would leave her to the coyotes to be eaten, or he would just slice her up. Tears rolled down his eyes. Luis could not stand the injustice; it reminded him of the abuse he'd been put through by so many who did not understand him. He stood up and whispered to the man that he might as well start with him because Luis would not allow him to take advantage of the girl. Nano woke up and went over to where they were. "What's going on?" he asked in Spanish. Demonio told him that there was no problem, that they were just in disagreement and that it was none of his business. Nano, not wanting to lose control, told them to be quiet. Nano went back to sleep.

By now the girl had buttoned her jeans back up and her brother was hugging her protectively. Demonio gave Luis a menacing look. He took the blunt side of a knife blade and swiped it across his own neck as he stared at Luis and said, "Cuidate carbon," – watch your back.

Luis could no longer sleep. He put his hands behind his head as a pillow and stared at the stars.

When they woke, the girl's brother came up to Luis; it was four in the morning and still dark. He thanked Luis for saving his sister, and made excuses for not standing up to Demonio. Luis told him it was all right, and said he didn't blame him, that he didn't know why he did it and that he normally wasn't that brave. The brother introduced himself in Spanish. "My name is Cuihtlahuac, they call me Wakas. This is my sister Chayo." She extended her hand to Luis, and he introduced himself. She said, "Rosario Fuentes, *gracias*." She thanked him for stepping in and helping her when her own brother couldn't.

The sun came up and it was unbearable. Demonio was chugging his second water bottle as Nano yelled at him to stop drinking. "*Aguanta guey!*" He told them they must conserve water because they still had a long way to go. They were huddled behind a small sand hill. In front of them was a dirt road which was frequented by Border Patrol vehicles; beyond that was several miles of flatland, low brush desert as far as the eye could see. There was nowhere to hide in the wide expanse, and behind the expanse was a big mountain range.

Nano explained that they would wait for the Border Patrol truck to pass, and when it did, they would have thirty minutes to haul their butts to those mountains, which were about three miles away. Once over the mountains, they would be only twenty miles from the outskirts of the nearest town: safety.

As they waited, they asked Nano about sensors and tricks that the Border Patrol used. Nano explained that he never showed them any of the twenty to thirty sensors he'd encountered and avoided only because he hadn't wanted to frighten them. Plus, he was tired as heck, as he put it in Spanish.

He shushed them, and they stayed still for two to three minutes. Sure enough a Border Patrol truck kicking up dust could be heard and then seen coming from afar. They were all scared and nervous. The truck was getting closer; Chayo started to breathe hard. She was afraid; she didn't think she could make it. Her brother pleaded with her to control herself. They were all afraid. They would be within fifty feet of the vehicle as it passed; they prayed that it wouldn't stop. Luis moved next to a very nervous Chayo. She was practically hyperventilating, so he began to tell her about his horses back at his father's ranch. "There was this one time," he began in Spanish. He told about the time when he was 12 years old, his father made him watch the horses because Luis had a way with them. Every now and then a neighboring ranch would report that they had lost a cow or a horse to a pack of wolves; the wolves came down from the sierra to hunt, but they mostly stuck to sheep or smaller animals. These were tough times, and the wolves were getting bolder, they were attacking large animals as a pack.

Luis was on watch one particular night when he heard the howls of the wolves as they cried in the night. He figured they were communicating their plan, calling the other wolves. He tried so hard to interpret what they were saying. Deep inside, Luis actually admired the wolf. He thought the wolf was an amazing animal and misunderstood, like himself. He could almost picture himself as a wolf out in the bitter winter cold, alone, with hunters on the prowl. However, his love for horses far outweighed the empathy he could feel for the *lobo*.

Realizing it was but a matter of time before the wolves came calling, he prepared himself. He heard the sounds of the horses getting nervous and was there with them, calming them with his soothing voice. All through the night the howls of the wolves cried out, and Luis calmly spoke to the horses, assuring them that they would be safe. He stayed with them until morning, until the sun came up; the wolves would return to their dens and the horses would be safe for one more night.

Luis calmly spoke to Chayo with the same soothing voice. He told her that fear was a normal response to danger and that it was okay to be scared. He told her he was scared too, but together, they would make it across that desert. He assured her that the Border Patrol would not get her because Nano would deliver them safely. She would be sipping cold soda pops in no time at all. He gripped her hand and told her to take a deep breath: Breathe in, breathe out, slow. The loud engine of the truck broke up the quiet peace of the lonely desert. A dispatch radio could be heard sending out messages in English. The truck passed by, and as soon as it was out of sight Nano yelled for them to run. *"Andale corran!"* He told them to run as fast as they could without stopping, without looking back.

Luis took Chayo's hand and pulled her along. Her feet wouldn't move and they fell behind; her brother had gone ahead. Luis looked her in the eyes and told her that he didn't want to die, that he was not leaving her side, and that if she didn't pick up her feet they would both be left alone in the desert. She realized what he was saying and slowly started to walk. He encouraged her by telling her she was fine and that the *migras* (immigration officers) were far away and that it wasn't so hard after all. She picked up the pace and soon both were in a full stride, running for freedom.

The rest of their party was ahead of them; they looked like tiny ants. Luis was worried that they might be spotted by the Border Patrol on its next pass, helicopters might be called, he didn't know how long it had been; they had been jogging for a long time. Chayo was out of breath. He looked back toward the Border Patrol trail, which was now about two miles away. He saw a small cloud of dust. It was the Border Patrol truck on its route back. He told her to lie down, as flat as she could. The soft dirt was unbearably hot; she did as she was told, she trusted him. Once the Border Patrol truck passed they make a break for the mountains to try to catch up to their party.

Fifteen minutes later they came to the rocky foot of the giant mountain. There were definitely many places to hide but also many places to fall, or find an unfriendly rattlesnake. The hulking mountain extended above the sky; it was a scary sight. Chayo's eyes widened as she saw what she had to climb. She regretted ever deciding to make the trip, and began to pray; she prayed hard. They started to hike up the hill; she had all but given up hope. She told Luis to give her brother messages for her because she didn't think she could make it that far. Luis reassured her that she would make it, with him. They would make it together.

Halfway up the mountain they stopped to rest. They sat on top of a giant rock, their feet dangling in the air; they could see Mexico behind them, beyond the mountain ranges, and they both began to imagine what might be going on in their respective towns. Luis wondered about his mother, how sad she must be. She had not wanted him to go, but he knew he could not stay, he had to leave. He saw his mother in front of him, saying, "Luisito, I made you this necklace, *para que te recuerdes de mi.*" (I made you this necklace so you can remember me.) She took a leather shoelace with a wooden pendant and tied it around his neck. He touched it with his right hand as if to say, "I will cherish it as if it were made of gold, *madrecita,*" but he didn't say anything.

Luis told Chayo that they must move on, but she refused to go any farther. She felt she would die there, and she began to cry. Chayo told him she had dropped her water bottle while running, so he gave her some of his. He gently tugged her and she slowly began the climb up to the top of the hill.

As they climbed, Luis continued to look back for Chayo to make sure she was still with him; he sang a song to encourage her and at the same time distract her from her misery. He pointed to a huge rock above and told her that it was the summit rock, and they were only a hundred yards away. She started to believe that she could make it. She had a new sense of encouragement. She continued her march up, and she began to sing the tune that Luis was singing to her. Luis looked back at her and smiled.

They reached the summit; it was the most beautiful place Luis had ever seen. They were both amazed at the beauty and humbled by the immense mountaintop; they both began to cry. It was a cry of happiness. They looked around toward the horizon, three hundred and sixty degrees around them. They turned and turned and turned; they began to laugh like two kids. *"Gracias Dios, Gracias!"* They yelled their thanks to God, they laughed, they hugged and then they cried some more. Although they were exhausted their spirits were refreshed with the beauty all around them, and with a renewed sense that all would be okay.

Luis told her that they must try to catch up and gain ground, that the way down would be much easier. They started the trek down; they saw the little city from above. He pointed and told her that they had made it. She laughed and cried at the same time. She was nervously excited, but mostly happy to be done with the horrible mountain hike. She was hot, thirsty and tired but continued to march down the steep, rocky terrain. She realized things about herself she had never known. She knew that she was tougher than she'd thought, but also that life itself was a cold, tough beast; she thanked God again.

It was getting dark and they were almost down the mountain; twenty-four hours had passed since they'd started their trek, and they had used up all their water, food, energy and spirit. They made it to the base of the mountain. They were so tired their legs could barely walk. Chayo begged for a rest stop, but before Luis could answer her, he fell to his knees after the sound of a loud thump and a malevolent laugh.

Demonio, who'd been lying in wait, had purposely fallen away from the leading pack and had been hiding behind a big boulder at the base of the mountain. Chayo tried to scream, but nothing came out of her mouth. She looked around desperately for somewhere to run. Her tired legs started to go when Demonio grabbed her; he manhandled her as if she were a rag doll. "I am going to bang the shit out of you, little whore! Where is your little girlfriend now, huh? Look, he's dead. I did that, and if you resist, you will join him after I'm done pumping you full of jelly," Demonio said with a rough voice.

Although there was nobody around for miles, he dragged her back by the rocks and tore off her blouse and bra. Her small breasts exposed, she tried to cover them in horror; he ripped off her jeans, threw her on the dirt and mounted her. He was in a frenzy, like a wild animal. She could only look up to the sky with watery eyes; she silently cried, then closed her eyes in shame.

He came inside her after a couple of minutes. "That's a good girl, you like that? That wasn't so bad, right? Little bitch!" Demonio got off on humiliating women. He flew up and away, his feet off the ground, and he landed in a cloud of dust. Luis had summoned all his strength and had pulled him off her. Luis turned towards the evil man to ensure he didn't try anything more. Demonio got back up and ran toward Luis with a flying midair kick that hit Luis right in the stomach; Luis flew back, landed hard on his behind.

Demonio took his knife out and ran towards Luis. Luis got up and barely missed the knife's fast swinging swipe; he moved about like a boxer in a gym, desperately trying to get Chayo to run for safety, but Chayo was in shock; she could not move. Luis searched for a rock or stick to repel the sharp edge of the knife. Luis anticipated the next knifing attempt, moving from side to side, barely missing the deadly blade. He zigged and he zagged; he kept moving while a tired Demonio began to huff and puff like a bull being toyed with by a matador.

With one last swing, Demonio hit his target; he hit Luis across the jaw with the fist that was holding the knife handle, then he went for a left hook. When Luis grabbed his hand and collar and used the man's own momentum to swing him toward a big cactus plant, Demonio screamed; he was stuck, but too tired and hurt to move.

Luis turned towards a horrified Chayo; Demonio was stuck in a frozen position, a prisoner of the cacti. "Are you okay?" Luis asked Chayo, but she couldn't speak, she was in shock, and she held herself with her arms. Luis began to approach her, to hug her and reassure her that everything was going to be fine. She looked at Luis with a blank, lifeless stare. Suddenly, her eyes widened in horror.

Luis was rammed like a football player unaware of a tackler from behind. His arms and legs flailed about as Demonio knocked him down again, except this time he wrestled himself on top of Luis, pinned Luis's arms with his knees, and began a series of left and right punches to Luis's face. Blood shot all over. Luis tried in vain to move his legs and get out of the deadly hold, but the hard punches were too much, knocking him out.

Demonio continued to pound the unconscious boy, the poor boy who loved horses, Luis's head flopping side to side, kicking up dirt and blood. Demonio was talking to him with every punch. "You...don't... mess... with... me... you... messed with... the wrong... mutha!" Suddenly, a loud, echoing sound of cracking skull and a splatter of red; Chayo smashed a huge rock onto Demonio's head. Demonio fell onto Luis like a baby lion cub sleeping on a tree branch.

Chayo rolled Demonio off of Luis. As Demonio was rolled onto his back, Chayo could see that his eyes had grayed over; he was dead. Blood was all around, red dirt clumps surrounding the perimeter; signs of a tremendous battle. Chayo garnered the strength and moved Luis away from the sun, into the only shade, behind the same big boulder where Demonio had been hiding earlier; there was a large plastic water container sitting on the dirt. Chayo immediately began to nurse her knight in shining armor; the worst, she thought, was finally over.

After several hours Luis awakened. It was dark and Chayo was asleep next to him behind the rock. He didn't know where he was; she woke up and began to tell him all that had happened earlier. They were hungry and had very little water left. They had some water that Demonio surely had stolen from the leading pack, who by now had written off the two; God knew where Chayo's brother was.

They fell asleep. They huddled together for warmth. Although the days were unbearably hot, the nights could get cold in the desert. They awoke at first light, it was 6 a.m. They began to walk towards where they remembered the town to be, but it was miles of desert as far as the eye could see. They were disoriented, not knowing where they were; they knew the mountain was south, so they headed the opposite direction for 10 miles. Luis saw a plume of smoke towards the east. There must have been somebody there. They were desperate, and they walked that way.

They walked for an hour, it must have been four miles. They saw a distant highway and a vehicle on fire. They approached to find the burning car a few hundred yards off the road; somebody must have needed to dispose of it, he told Chayo. They walked toward the road. As they walked they saw a vehicle approaching, a van, it was the Disciples of Jehovah the Lamb of God Church in Christ missionary van en route to its church, which was nearby. They stopped to offer assistance; in the end, they picked up Luis and Chayo and drove them into the city, where they fed them and provided them with anything they could. One of the people who welcomed them inside knew the scenario all too well. "I believe one of your comrades is already here, I will take you to him."

They were led down a hallway to the back rooms of the big church; it was a maze of sorts. They opened a door and entered a big room that had cots lined up against the walls. They saw Chayo's brother sitting on a cot with his elbows on his knees and his hands covering his face. "Chava!" Chayo cried out to her brother. Chava immediately looked up and ran toward his sister. "I thought I had lost you, Chayo, I'm so sorry!" He looked at Luis. "Thank you again, sir, I don't know your name. Well I don't remember...." Luis interrupted. "Luis is my name, and it's okay, I wanted her to be safe. Anyone would have done the same."

They sat and drank the hot coffee and ate the sandwiches that the good Christians had served them; they talked about the whole incident. Chava told them in great detail how Demonio had discovered that one of the immigrants crossing was a mule; he was carrying a kilo of cocaine. After they descended the big mountain, they heard a commotion. They looked back and saw Demonio wrestling the young mule to the ground, taking his backpack and water jug. Demonio stood in defiance as the others went back to help. He withdrew a knife and dared them to try something stupid, as he put it.

He took out the packet of the white powder, stabbed it with his knife, took out a pile of the cocaine, then proceeded to snort it with his left nostril; he repeated the same thing with his right nostril. Demonio let out a scream like the devil, then ran back towards the mountain with the backpack and the mule's water jug. The brother told them the story of how Demonio went AWOL and they had no choice but to leave him behind. Luis realized why Demonio was so crazed, his eyes glazed over like a maniac.

They stayed the night at the church and early the next morning all three arose, thanked the man in charge of the facility and asked him to thank the entire congregation for their hospitality. They were dropped off at the bus terminal. Chava and Chayo headed to Tennessee to stay with a friend of the family, and Luis headed to a horse ranch in South Carolina that he'd heard about from one of his father's ranch hands.

As Luis finished his story Psyko piped in, "Man, that ain't nothing, man. You think that's bad, *ese,* you had a mom that loved you and people that cared for you. I wish I had a father. I wish I had a father that hit me, at least somebody would be recognizing my existence." Psyko stopped suddenly, knowing he was releasing his inner person, something he never did. Reymundo caught the moment. He knew Psyko had a story to tell, he knew there was more to the crazy-looking gangbanger. "Well, at least tell us, man, a little, so we know who we dealing with," said Reymundo.
Psyko began a string of hateful, condescending words.

Cholo

"As far back as I can remember, I always had a gun in my hand. I'll take out any crazy *loco* that wants a piece of me! When the Maravilla fools tried to take out my little homie Sieks, who had his back? Me, that's who! I sprayed those *putos* with seven pounds of lead! And that goes for all you wetbacks, prom queen bitch, *putos*, and an old oxidized son of a bitch! You think you have something in common with me cause you're Mexicans? Forget that!" Eriberto Montiel Garibay, AKA Psyko, was true to his word and to his nickname. He was a ruthless killer with no morals or compassion for the weak. He wore an Oakland Raiders jersey even though he was from LA.

Raised in the streets of Los Angeles since his mother had overdosed on heroin, he only had his hood and his homies, and anyone who disrespected him found themselves four feet separated from their severed head in a shallow grave behind the Fosters Freeze on Atlantic Boulevard. His shaved head was now had a five o'clock shadow that was starting to cover all the tattoos on his scalp.

"Why are you so angry, *cholo*?" asked Reymundo. "What would your mother say if she heard you talk that way in front of a lady?" Psyko gave Reymundo a look that could pierce a bulletproof vest. "You don't need to be bringing up my *jefita* (mom), *pinche viejo oxidao* (damned oxidized old man)." Psyko turned away; he really did not want to get into it with an old man, and he thought Reymundo a pretty cool old dude. He had not thought about his mother in so many years. He couldn't, he'd refused to even think about her. But he couldn't stop now, since Mundo had brought her memory back to life, so he put his head down, hoping nobody would notice, and broke it down in his head. He began to tell the story.

He pictured himself at 10 years old, walking home from school, backpack around his shoulder, him and his little brother Jorge, who everyone called Coquiyo. Coquiyo was distracted, at 5 years old everything caught his attention. "Erik, are we, uhm, going to watch the … Hey, look how I cut the flower! Whoa, d'you see that, Erik?

Uhm, are we going to watch Pokémon or the *Chavo del Ocho*, if the TV's still there?"

"Maybe, after we get done with homework."
Arriving at the house, Eriberto was worried as he saw the curtains were drawn, she only did that when she needed privacy, which only meant one thing: She was shooting up. But why were they still drawn? She usually did the deed and promptly opened the curtains so as to not draw suspicion. He had a very uneasy feeling as he approached the gate. The twenty steps to the porch seemed like a mile. He slowly crept along the concrete path that led to the steps.

The cement was so cracked it resembled an elephant's ear. Within each crack lay used needles, needles left over from junkies, his own mother's friends who shot up at night.
He went to open the door but it was locked, so he knocked angrily, alerting his mother that this was unacceptable. He waited for her to open the door and then knocked as hard as he could. As he thought about what to do, a police car slowly passed.

The officer inside the squad car made eye contact with the boy and stopped. Eriberto quickly looked away, causing the patrol officer to go on about his business. They both sat on the makeshift swing hanging from the branch of an old tree at the side of the house. That's when he saw the open window.

"Coquiyo, *ven*! I'm going to lift you up to the side window, okay? Then you open the door and we'll watch the *Chavo del Ocho*, I promise."

"Okay, Erik, *Chavo del Ocho*. Okay, Erik," responded an obedient Coquiyo. Eriberto gave him a boost. He shoved his little brother up and into the window until he heard a "Whoa," and then a thump; this caused Eriberto to laugh. He ran around the house and waited at the front door. He waited patiently for about a minute, then he heard the familiar music coming from the television inside the house.

"Pum, pum pum pum, pum pum pum; pum pa da da da da da pum pum pum... *El Chavo Del Ocho!*" sang the TV. "Damn it, Coquiyo, you forgot about me," Eriberto mumbled. He rapped on the door, which was covered in crackled paint, as hard as he could. He heard a series of little steps followed by the unlocking of the door, and *voila*, it was open. Coquiyo jetted back to the shag carpeting, sliding like a ballplayer into second base and ending up in an upright kneeling position, his back at ninety degrees to the floor, his eyes fixed on the television. Eriberto heard his mother's television coming from her room.

Eriberto slowly walked through the hallway. The empty rooms with clothes scattered about the floors were a normal thing, but why was his mother's door closed? Eriberto knocked on the door. "Mom?" He turned the knob and let himself in; the bed was unmade, as usual. The movie *The Outsiders* was on TV, the Stevie Wonder song "Stay Gold" was playing.

He figured she must have been in the bathroom; he went to check and that's when he found her. She was slumped on the toilet seat, eyes grayed over, lifeless. Her skin was blue and her lips were white. Her arm was stuck out as if to say, "Gimme five." A needle was stuck in her blue arm; she had overdosed.

Eriberto removed the needle and threw it on the floor, and grabbed his mother by the shoulders trying to wake her up. "Come on, Mom, wake up, Coquiyo needs you, Mom, come on Mom." He put his little arms around her as her head slumped onto his shoulder. He hugged her lifeless body as tight as he could and cried a sob that came from within the deepest part of his innocent soul. He stayed that way for a few minutes, then released her as her body fell back against the porcelain and her head dangled back.

He could not move; he was frozen. He wanted to run but his legs didn't answer the request. He finally took two steps back, trembling, tears in his eyes. The pain pierced his soul like a heavy needle going through leather. His entire being collapsed. His biggest fear in the world was now a reality. His mother was dead.

As he sat in the back of the squad car Coquiyo played with an action figure as if it were an airplane. "Hulk Hogan flying tru da air, vroom!" he would say as he made figure eights in the air. Eriberto looked out the window toward his house one last time. He promised himself he would never hurt again. The wound to his soul would form the thickest scar tissue that it could. He didn't even want to feel again. He wanted to be as soulless as that Hulk Hogan action figure flying through the air. Then and only then could he be free at last. He looked at his little brother Coquiyo talking to himself and playing with his toy.

Eriberto looked over at both sides of the street toward the neighboring houses. All the nosy neighbors had gathered; some weighed in, others commented, still others chuckled. Eriberto saw the neighbor bullies standing with their mothers and their fathers, the same kids who'd laughed at his ripped shoes, the secondhand clothes, the empty lunch box he carried to pretend he was normal; they had ridiculed him on a daily basis, yet they were never able to make him cry, and he would be damned if they would see him crying now. He heard a neighbor tell the cops about his mother's drug use and all-night junkie parties for the whole world to hear.

Neighbors looked at him with curiosity, some glad to know that the disturbing family on Welfare had finally reaped what they had sown. Eriberto breathed hard to keep himself from crying. *No, not today*, he thought, but the tears were filling his little eyes faster than he could support them, and then it happened – the big, fat tears rolled down his little pink cheeks nonstop. He tried his best to order his eyes to stop, to no avail; he was mad at himself that he'd let them see him cry.

They rode on their last trip together to Child Protective Services. He was sure he would never see his brother again.

Reymundo saw that the young, tough gangster was getting emotional; everyone was quiet listening to Psyko's story. Nelly and Luis had tears in their eyes. Pretty Boy was wiping his eyes. "Damn allergies, this dry desert is killing me," he said.
Reymundo began to continue the story of the Aztecs; this would surely change the somber mood. "Let me continue the story of our forefathers," he said.

"Yeah, yeah, that's a good idea," remarked Pretty Boy.

The Rise and Fall of Aztatlan III – The Jaguar and the *Coyotl*

On one particular evening, Mexitli, the king of Aztatlan, gathered the elders and warrior chiefs and said unto them, "A rogue jaguar has taken another one of our children. Not even the Chichimec with their barbaric ways come into our village with such contempt. How can we allow this animal, though sacred he may be, to take our children in sacrifice? We must put together a unit of our bravest men and go about the wilderness and hunt down this beast."

Now this was no ordinary beast. This jaguar was one of the oldest and biggest and most daring of all jaguars; he was the alpha male cat that dominated an area around the coast. The son of the king, little Tenoch, was listening to this meeting as he hid under the leather hides, and was inspired to set off on his own to slay the wild beast that taunted his people. Surely he would be praised as a hero; his father would be so proud.

He took with him his sharp obsidian blade, his *hacha* (axe), and a spear, and went on his way in the evening. Tenoch was but 14 years old at the time, but he had the heart of ten men and the courage of fifty warriors. He was his father's favorite son. He went to the place where the Peyotl was abundant and collected three Peyotl buttons. He then trekked the whole night until he heard the *coyotl* howls in the night, an awful sound. He waited until the *coyotl* made the sound of the call of the feast.

They had slain a young dear and were feasting.
Young Tenoch, wearing a fierce disguise, screaming and howling, ran into the feasting band of *coyotl*, and the *coyotl* were so perplexed, they knew that this beast was more fierce than they were, so they ran off. Tenoch took the carcass and ran off into the night. He grinded the Peyotl buttons on a flat rock and put the pulp in the meat. He also doused the meat with the juices of the Peyotl until it was soaked.

Tenoch then found the jaguar's tracks and began his midnight chase for the fierce beast. He heard the sounds of animals in the night. He set the meat out on a rock near a tree the jaguars were known to frequent, and waited nearby for the beast to arrive. He had smeared his body with a pungent flower and urine mixture.

Now, back at the camp, Mexitli the chief was interrogating his younger son about the whereabouts of Tenoch. "You must tell me. It's dark and he is nowhere to be found. If you know where your older brother is, tell me now, or I will personally flog you with seven, no ten, prickly reeds." The younger brother cried but admitted that he knew where his brother was.

"I walked into the room where we set our camp. Tenoch was gathering his lance and his leather pack that Nana gave him. I asked him where he was going. He put a finger against his lips and said that he would skin me alive if I told you. I asked him if I could go, that I would be very good. He said it was dangerous and that I was better off here. He said that the jaguar was going to meet his end. Then he left."

Mexitli got down on his knees and began to howl a cry of pure sorrow. "My God, oh, what has he done? He will surely meet his death." He stood up and ordered all his elders to appoint a group of night hunters who would go out and find the boy.
"With all respect to you, great leader, it is far from the full moon and very dark, we will not find him now, but we will make our best attempt," answered one of them. They consoled the chief, who had his hands raised in the air as if to signal the Sun God for help.

Away from the camp, Tenoch huddled and stayed as still as possible. He heard the familiar sound of the jaguar's prey cackling and howling in the midnight moon, alerting each other to the jaguar's presence. The large cat appeared in a small clearing surrounded by rocks, trees, cacti, and other flora. When the feline approached the tainted meat, it first looked around as if it knew it was being watched. It circled the meat, approached it, sniffed it, and then turned away, towards a crouching Tenoch, hiding behind an elevated boulder, camouflaged in branches.

Tenoch's plan was to wait until the animal ate the meat, stalk the animal until it became disoriented, then pounce on it with his lance. The plan seemed perfect. However, jaguars are predators, not scavengers. The cat leaped at the young hunter and with a powerful swipe knocked the boy off the massive stone, the lance falling by his side. The jaguar leaped down to devour his prey, and when he did, he let out a horrific, screaming growl that could be heard throughout the wilderness.

Tenoch had grabbed his pointed lance and set it at an angle towards the leaping animal, and the jaguar landed right on it; the lance pierced the jaguar's throat. The animal squirmed about the ground and tried to run but couldn't breathe; it was horrible sound. Tenoch was horrified but relieved that he had survived against all odds. Still in shock, Tenoch stood above the beast who must have been seven feet long, not including the tail. Tenoch's heart was still racing.

He made a sort of bed with sticks and branches and used it to drag the animal back to the village. He arrived at sunrise. He found the elders at the edge of the village and they ran towards him; his father, with open arms, was crying, for he thought his oldest son had surely perished.

Psyko was now inspired with this story of *La Raza* and went into deep thought. He remembered his own challenges and the mistakes he had made along the way. He thought that if he'd had his father growing up, he might not have been inside that van. His father had come to America illegally with his mom when Psyko was only 4 years old; Coquiyo was born a year later.

The People of the Sun – *La Raza*

A 1974 Chevy Impala Glasshouse lowrider cruised the barrio of East
Los Angeles, Rage Against the Machine's "People of the Sun"
playing on the stereo at an unhealthy decibel level. A thug with a
shaved head rode shotgun, bouncing from the rough ride of the
hydraulics. He was wearing a blue bandana wrapped around his
head, tied in the front *a la* Tupac. He was wearing black wraparound
sunglasses. As the car cruised by a series of abandoned buildings,
houses, winos, crack whores and walls tagged with graffiti, one
could see the "Psyko" tag on a wall of a nondescript building. The
driver, a dark Mexican they called Chino, was wearing a grey
lowrider brim hat.

The car slowed, then stopped at a stop sign where some girls were
standing at a corner. The Impala did a series of hydraulic dances then
finished with a slow and steady drop until the frame touched the
ground. Hydraulics could be vividly heard, like an urban dance of
courtship. The girls were impressed, and the car's two occupants,
acting like it was no big deal, raised the car back to normal level,
then Chino suddenly pumped the hydraulics to lift the car up like a
four-by-four truck; they slowly cruised forward.

As the car turned a corner the two occupants discussed something as
Psyko fiddled with an object on his lap. The driver was explaining in
detail about an incident regarding his girlfriend; she gave him such a
hard time and he was getting tired of her. Psyko raised his hands to
shoulder level and continued rolling a joint; he licked the edge and
finished; the precisely rolled blunt was shaped like a big, long
Bugles corn chip. Psyko sparked the doobie, took several tokes, then
took two more. He passed it to the driver, who was saying, "Let me
hit that shit, Psyko." He grabbed the fatty excitedly but did not stop
talking. Psyko looked out the open window and blew out the smoke
in a long, smooth, steady stream that formed into a cloud and drifted
into the open air.

They were arriving at their destination. They pulled towards the curb in slow motion. Four gang bangers were playing a game of craps; one knelt on the sidewalk, two crouched with hands on their knees like old-time catchers, watching the throw of the dice. The fourth one, standing, turned to see what was behind him, and he quickly signaled to the others who got up as they all turned towards the oncoming car, reaching for their waistbands. Psyko turned his bandana around to cover his face, looking like an old-time Western bank robber. He stepped out of the car in three swift motions and fired a series of four precision shots; *bang, bang, bang, bang.* One by one the four guys fell to the concrete like dominoes while their guns dropped to the ground. They were dead, each with a gunshot to the head.

"You are one bad muther!" said the driver with admiration. Psyko responded, "Oh yeah? Come on, let's go over to the guy." They headed west towards the LA skyline, no music playing. Psyko told the driver, "*Oye,* homes, put that Pink Floyd CD on, no?" The driver fussed with the CD above his sun visor. "Here it is, Pink Floyd *Dark Side of the Moon* coming up for the most ruthless assassin in the Southland, Heh-Hah! Man, you're like a crazy genius Pink Floyd-listening killer and shit, huh? Hey man I wrote a rap song about getting high you want to hear it?" asked Chino. "Orale man fire away." responded Psyko. Chino began a beatbox drum beat then spewed out some lyrics:

I'm under I'm under I'm under I'm under the influence
I'm under the influence, more vapors then a sauna
But that is the only way to smoke marijuana
Under the smoke tree, I'm falling to my knees
I'm smoking, and toking, and burning up trees
I'm under the influence, Salvia Divinorum
I'm getting more buzzed than bees in a swarm
I'm under I'm under I'm under I'm under the influence
U Damn right Skippy like a jar a peanut butta
My words just stutter, I mutter, I flutter, like a welcome back kotter
Suffering succotash, sicker than siccophant,

faster than sexy sour Sanskrit seeking psychopath
I'm under the influence, peyote mescaline
Sipping more lean, then a crsytal meth fiend
I'm under I'm under I'm under I'm under the influence
I'm under the influence I drank a fifth a Vodka,
I stagger with more swagger when I say "What the Fodka?"
Aesthetic, Pathetic, hermetic, energetic
It's hectic, I wrecked It, but never confessed it,
I'm under the influence, a fun guy Psilocybin
I'd rather take the bus cause I ain't drunk driving
I'm under I'm under I'm under I'm under the influence
I'm under the influence, but don't be dissing
Tetra hydro cannabinol, I'll be be pissing
Under the influence more faded than your shirt
Crush'em down and snort them up then chase it with a perc
I'm under the influence and I could barely stand
Your constant ass bitching just made me drop a grand
I'm under I'm under I'm under I'm under the influence
Killing purple serum, making me delirum,please not so loud, that I
just can't hear'em
Drop'em like it's hot, gonna smoke some pot, are you gonna pass a
test, I think not
Police shots firing, rolling with the siren, ran into restaurant, ooh
Burger King is Hiring,
Like an open forum, talk till you bore'em, take a hike and pick me up
Salvia divinorum
Chase me like I'm running bare, underwearon the floor'em
I'm under I'm under I'm under I'm under the influence

Psyko really liked the song and complemented his partner "Man you
got skills bro, you can't shoot a gun but you can rap ese!" They
arrived at a house with boarded windows and a condemned sign in
the front. They carefully walked to the back of the house through the
side yard. Once inside, Psyko sat on an old, ripped sofa while the
driver dramatically described the events that had occurred to the guy.
A skinny tweeker-looking guy mixed and blended, measured and
filled chemicals into beakers; it was an underground meth lab.

A girl with a piercing was smoking some crystal meth from a piece of aluminum foil. She took a big hit, held it in as long as she could, and then, when she could no longer hold it, her breath exploded with an exhaled mixture of burned CO_2 and remnants of crystal meth which vaporized and blended into the toxic cloud in the otherwise musty room. Her eyes completely glazed over, rolling to the back of her head; she closed them and began to rock slowly from side to side as if listening to a jazz ensemble playing in her head. The Pink Floyd was still playing in Psyko's head, his eyes off into the distant haze; he was trying to make sense of his life.

The girl crawled up to Psyko, slowly like a stripper on all fours; she knelt in front of him, sat up between his knees, put her hand in the area of his crotch. She crouched over him and reached toward his buckle. He didn't even look down. From behind her, you could see her head go down, and then up, then down again, up, down, up and down, a little faster. She was moaning with a stuffed mouth; she gagged a bit.

He looked down and saw her; she was caressing and stroking his pistol, the one he had just unloaded on the gang bangers, she had swallowed the entire barrel, her mouth pressed up against the trigger point. Psyko shook his head, removed her from his weapon, and gently shoved her away.

He put the gun back into his waistband. She wiped drool from her mouth with the back of her hand. She was still kneeling but now she was tilted to the side, leaning on her right hand in an erotic pose. She looked back, eyes fixed on Psyko as he walked away. He was the embodiment of everything she wanted in a man. He walked away. She picked up the piece of foil off the floor and got her lighter, and continued to smoke the meth.

The bedroom door opened. A strange white guy hurried out, and a hardcore older Mexican stepped out briefly. "Psyko! *Caile.*" Psyko gave him an old school *veterano* handshake, then they embraced and went into the room.

Back inside the car, the driver and Psyko drove away from the Maravilla housing project. The driver started to comment on what he thought had just occurred. "The guy is pretty cool, huh? Man, I saw that fine little tweeker bitch blow you, man… Gotta say, you're quick, man… Don't worry, man, I'd a hit that too if she wouldn't have been all over you."

"Man, she put that long barrel in her mouth; she took it all in, *ese*, what am I supposed to do, discharge my weapon all over her face? Shoot my bullets in her mouth? Lucky for her I didn't!" Psyko chuckled.

The driver, all hot and bothered, replied, "Oh yeah? Man, you're having some kind of day, huh? Hey man, my girl's got a friend that's always asking about you and my girl's like yeah, man, bring your homie Psyko over, man. She thinks you don't like her, *ese*."

"I can't, man, I gotta go see my Carnal, Coquiyo, you know he thinks he has to watch over me, thinks I'm too crazy. I already lost him once, and no matter what it takes I ain't gonna lose him again."

"I respect that shit, *ese, la familia primero,* huh?"
"Shut up, ey, you know you all my *familia* now. Yeah, he's my *familia* by blood, but all these years apart, we really went different ways. I think his wife is scared of me. His baby daughter, man, she my world, man, she's got eyes like my…" He paused for a moment. "She's got beautiful eyes, hypnotic eyes, she digs me though. Yo, man, stop right here by the Koreans, I got to get something." Psyko bought a cheap plastic fake Barbie, the kind they called Schmarbies. It was about a foot long, right off the container ship from China, and for the bargain basement price of only two dollars.

Chino drove Psyko to Coquiyo's house. Psyko was about to get out when he got a call. He listened intently to the caller and said, "I'm with Chino right now, I could be there in a half hour... Okay, we'll leave right now, see you in ten minutes." He looked at Chino and said, "There's some kind of problem. Brujo sounds scared, man, I never heard him sound like that. We better go to the club." He apologized to his brother, who was waiting on the porch with his daughter, little Ariel.

She got down from her father's arms and ran towards her uncle. "Uncle, uncle!" shouted the little angel.
Psyko gave her the doll, which the little girl accepted with eyes wide and a smile that could melt your heart. "For me?" she asked.

"Yeah, *mija,* now go play with her," Psyko said. He addressed his younger brother: "I just got a call from work, I'm sorry I can't stay," he said.

"Man, you do this all the time. How many times have I told you, man, I'm your family. I'm your blood. Those guys, they're going to get you into a mess of trouble some day. Come on, man, Lupita is waiting inside. She made *caldo siete mares* (seven seas soup), at least have a bowl. It's your favorite," Coquiyo pleaded. "We were separated for fifteen years, man, we have a lot to catch up on, bro!"

"I'm sorry, Coquiyo, tell Lupe that I will make it up to her. I will do the landscaping here or something, I'll paint the house. I will come back as soon as this thing is done, I'll eat the *caldo* cold cause she makes the best in town. I really am sorry, homie, I have to go."
Psyko left hurriedly and jumped into Chino's lowrider, which sped off towards Montebello Boulevard.

Club Thirteen was a seedy hangout on Montebello Boulevard in the heart of East Los Angeles. The club was a front for the largest Mexican gang in LA; it was where the shots were called. It looked like a regular dive bar with illegals and *paisas* drinking the night away, but behind the façade was a ruthless organization that controlled the lucrative black market in the Southland.

Chino drove to Montebello Boulevard and arrived at the club in ten minutes, as his partner had promised. When they got there, they were flanked by armed thugs and escorted inside. They went to the back room, which was suddenly blocked by three armed gangsters who had previously been pretending to select songs from the jukebox. "He's gotta see Brujo, come on, man!" Chino barked at the three sentinels. They knocked a series of coded knocks and the door opened. They all went inside, and the man behind the desk lit up a big joint. He puffed it hard and sucked it in deep, then exhaled while closing his eyes. He puffed again, then puffed twice more and passed it to Psyko.
"The hit you did today…" Brujo was still coughing from the hit of marijuana. "That was an illegal hit."

Psyko stopped hitting the joint and exhaled. Smoke came out of his mouth as he talked. "No way, it was sanctioned. I got it straight from Yogi in the Maravilla Projects, you know, the meth house," replied Psyko.

"We made a truce this morning. No more hits, no more drive-bys. We met this morning. Whoever gave you the green light set you up, man. Yogi is in the back room and he swears that he didn't authorize that hit. He says that was your own personal vendetta for that rapist son of a bitch, who did deserve to die, but it was still an unauthorized hit."

"So, now what, Brujo? You gonna turn me over to those guys after I been so loyal? I lived and breathed the colors of my barrio and this is how I end up, like a punk?" Psyko said.

"Nobody, I mean nobody, will deny that you have been the most loyal straight-up soldier ever in the history of this organization. You are a stone cold assassin, but! You messed up also. You should have verified the hit as usual, and you let your anger for the rapist get the best of you. We got a piece of shit that didn't deserve to live off the street, but still, I repeat, it was not sanctioned by the organization. We have to turn you over to them.

That rapist was the younger brother of a shot-caller. He wants your ass or he will break the truce. I got it from way up high that we can't afford to lose this truce. Both gangs are connected now, and our power will reign over all Califas, but you won't be around to see that, brother. I'm sorry, I truly am, but you messed up, not me. I was able to get Chino off on a pardon because he didn't pull the trigger, but you will be delivered. Take him away."

Brujo put his head down and brushed his hands in the air, gesturing to his men to remove Psyko. They zip tied his wrists and drove him to the heart of the Maravilla Projects right in front of a veteran known as Night Owl. As fast as he was dropped out of the moving vehicle, he was picked up off the street and taken to a garage that quickly closed. There, seven guys awaited the boss. One guy punched Psyko in the jaw and said, "You killed four of my homies and now you're going to suffer."

He was interrupted by another who yelled, "He's here!" The garage door opened slowly, only halfway this time, as a big, old, bald, tattooed man crouched to get in. Psyko kicked the menacing guy in the balls and slid under as fast as he could with his hands still zip tied. The thugs took chase; some got in cars.

Psyko jumped over a three-foot fence like an Olympian and ran through an enclosed yard. He ran towards the back as he reached for his *filero,* which he always kept in his back pocket. He ran towards an alley but immediately jumped another fence; he avoided the streets and alleys where he could be spotted. He was able to pull the knife out and cut the zip tie halfway. Before he dropped it he continued running, then he put both hands on the point of a fence and pulled as hard as he could, which broke the zip tie the rest of the way. He ran for his life. He heard the sound of screeching tires and grabbed an iron stake that had been buried in the dirt to hold a wooden fence plank.

He ran with the stake in his hands onto Whittier Boulevard. The two cars arrived and the thugs got out of their cars but didn't fire any shots. They attacked him, and he attacked all of them. He stabbed one thug with his iron makeshift lance in the side of his torso, barely missing his liver; the young bald man went down. The sirens and lights of approaching police cars scared the rest of them away, but before Psyko could run the police had surrounded him, weapons drawn. He put his hands up and got on his knees next to the squirming and crying young man who was grabbing his bloody side, inhaling and exhaling profusely.

"Freeze!" the officers yelled. They loaded Psyko into the back of a police car and called an ambulance for his victim.
After three days in the county jail during which he did not cooperate with his appointed attorney, Psyko has his day in court. His contempt for the law did not help his case, and the judge did not see the young thug as a type to be easily rehabilitated. The judge read the file on the young Latino rebel. As far as the system knew, Psyko had many offenses but none was serious. He had never been caught on a murder; this was an attempted murder charge. The attorney argued for self-defense, but Psyko's gang affiliation quickly did away with that plea.

The judge looked at a tattooed Psyko, who was looking away. "So, you're bad ass, you like to show how tough you are? You could have killed that young man and you would be here looking at a murder rap. Let's see how tough you are going to be in your new home for the next three years. I am going sentence you to three years at Chino State Prison, after which you will be deported to your home country in Mexico." The judge sounded the gavel, and Psyko was escorted away in chains. He was loaded into a big grey bus known as the Grey Goose.

Psyko was escorted in a line of convicts into the prison. Many faces glared from within their own cells at the procession; marked men, doomed men. Men who would spend the rest of their lives caged inside the system howled and yelled profanities; they said things about the new arrivals' chastity, and how they would possess it by force if necessary. They were black, brown, white, Asian. They seemed to stick together by ethnicity. There were three Hispanic gangs, one that controlled the northern part of the state, one that controlled the southern part, and one from Central America, the most ruthless gang of all which was aligned with the southern gang. There were two white gangs: the Redneck Rebellion and Hitler's Hit Men. The black gangs included the African Syndicate of Assassins and the United Black Front.

Psyko was unshackled and pushed into his cell, the loud sound of the metal doors signaling the start of Psyko's new life. His cellmate, a young black man, was reading an adult magazine. He nonchalantly spoke. "You better request another cell, essay. I don't want no brown shit stinking up my house. Yeah, dis is my house, and if you stay you gonna be my bitch!" Psyko threw the blankets and linens that had been given to him and began pounding on the young black man's face while he was still lying down. The magazine went flying, pages fluttering like a pigeon taking flight. Blood gushed all over Psyko's face and prison-issued top. The black man never had a chance.

You could hear the population start up like animals in a jungle; they cheered on. "You gone die, you mutha!" they yelled. "You better watch yo back, *ese*, you dead!" still others warned. "Mess him up, young *ese*! We got yo back, *vato!*" cheered the brown brothers. The alarms sounded and the guards arrived to the cell running. They opened the cell. There must have been twelve guards, pistols drawn. Batons flew at Psyko's head.

"Oh, you bad, huh? You want to start fast, huh? Well, let's see how bad you are when we put you in the yard with the UBF and the ASA!" They called the medics; the young black man was covering his face, bloodied. Psyko was placed in solitary for two weeks.

He sat alone in a tiny cell in solitary with no windows or clocks or visitors. It was enough to drive a man crazy, and Psyko was no exception. He hadn't wanted to do what he did, but he knew this was not the street, he couldn't show any weakness, especially to a black man. He had to show that if anyone was going to mess with him, it wasn't going to be a cakewalk; he was no punk. The only thing that kept him sane was the lyrics in his head, lyrics that he wrote off the top of the dome, as he put it, whenever he was stressed.

Don't don't don't don't you break the code
Cause I won't won't won't take this anymore
I got an eight oh eight in the six one nine so I
smoked the four two oh now I'm really feeling real
fine
Crazy whack funky like a lunatic, fitty one fitty if you
real sick
Too many in my head and they can't bail me out,
they talkin all at once make me scream and shout
Just a lunatic walkin, talkin to myself, just musical
prodigy givin em some hell, so
Don't don't don't don't you break the code
Cause I won't won't won't take this anymore
Great balls a fire, I'm getting real tired, but I rather
be this way, then be all kinds of wired, cause
A two six one or a three eleven will make your head
explode like a one eight seven,
If you're gonna break the law with a four eight four,
don't five oh two, then come running to my door
Cause you're thinking I'm your hero, like my boy
Shapiro, but you got me all wrong, I'm just a ten five
zero
Don't don't don't don't you break the code
Cause I won't won't won't take this anymore.

When he was taken out of solitary, he got word that he was a marked man. He was green-lighted by the local gangs. He stayed in his cell, knowing that his days were numbered. He went through the first six months getting beat downs every day, but he was still alive. Every day, he felt it would be his last day alive. One day when the book cart passed – it passed every day – he finally decided to take out some books.

He selected a Bible and a book about the mighty Aztec Empire. Not being much of a reader, he got frustrated a lot, but he never gave up. The books took his mind off his pending death. He never snitched or participated in any other inmate beatings.

After eight months, a guard came to his cell. "Eriberto Montiel Garibay." The guard mispronounced his name. "Well, what do you know? They're letting you out. Looks like you've leached enough out of our system. We have no room in the prisons as it is, you're getting deported." Psyko, relieved, made the sign of the cross. He had survived. He'd been green-lighted for death by the prison gangs, but he was now being released. Still paranoid, he avoided celebrating inside, knowing that there was still much to endure until he would be free.

He was loaded into a van with four pasianos from Mexico and driven to the Blythe Detention Facility. There, he was given clothes by the nuns who visited. He saw a nun approach a big older guy who looked like he had the weight of the world upon him. Psyko wondered about this guy. He thought his own father must be that age, and wondered where he could be.

They stayed at the detention facility for three days before they were loaded onto an INS bus. On the bus, the older man, wearing a baseball cap, offered the seat next to him to the young *vato*. Psyko refused it without a word. He remembered when he was 5 years old; he remembered his father. He went back to take the seat. The big man talked a lot about salvation; Psyko listened but didn't pick up a word.

They arrived at the Arizona facility, where they were given food and water. An INS officer, needing two more bodies for a special San Diego trip, picked them both out of the line and put them onto an awaiting van. "Just give me him and him." The officer pointed at

Psyko and Reymundo; they were loaded in the van heading to the Port of Entry at San Ysidro via San Diego.

El Malinchista – The First Bathroom & Water Break

"Get the hell out! All you damn wetbacks get out! You think I feel
sorry for you, prom queen bitch? You think I have to give you food,
water, humanitarian aid? Well, you don't know Jack, ha!" Jack
Gutierrez was probably the meanest Border Patrol agent this side of
the Rio Grande. A true *pocho* (a Hispanic who doesn't speak
Spanish, or speaks it poorly), he had a deep-rooted contempt for
undocumented aliens, except of course when they came in the form
of beautiful young Latinas.

He hated Mexicans but loved Mexican food, especially Tex-Mex,
which had been his favorite food growing up in Texas. He was a
miserable diabetic man who constantly cheated on his diet with
sugary snacks, which aggravated his condition and caused him to
limp. He was more confused than anyone in that van. "Come on,
prom queen, get the hell out, it's prom night!" He laughed a hearty
whiskey laugh as he barreled towards the back of the van, limping,
banging on the metal screen of the window where Nelly was seated
at the rear. He amused himself by degrading the cargo and rattling
their nerves every chance he got, and he would get a lot of chances
on this trip.

They were allowed to sit under a tree as they took turns using the
restroom. Nelly spoke to Reymundo. "You know those stories of the
Aztecs? Are they true? I could almost imagine that scenario, you
know? My father always spoke about our supposed roots, he even
gave me some stupid Aztec name I hate, and I go by Nelly. But he
never told me like you told us. My father didn't know much about
the history of his culture, and I only know what I was forced to learn
in school, which I saw as a fairy tale. But you sure have a way with
words; you should write a book." Reymundo just laughed.

Officer Jack growled more profanities and loaded the men and
women onto the van, slamming the door behind them.
He shook the window screen and banged it with his baton like a
drum once again and started to sing, "Aye, aye, aye, aye, I am the

Frito bandito!" He laughed so hard his whole belly moved up and down. "Frito bandito!" He kept singing and strumming his baton, shaking his head, thinking himself so clever.

As they drove off, Nelly was obviously upset. Luis tried to console her. "*Estupido!* He doesn't even know how the song goes. You know how it goes, right, Nelly?"
"No, not really. I never heard it. What's it about, Ranas?" she asked him.

"It's about you." He sat up, excited and happy that she was responding to his coos. "A dark-haired beauty from the sierra with big black eyes and a mole next to her mouth like Marilyn Monroe. Reymundo, *dame el bajo no?*" he said to Reymundo, requesting a bass line. He then began to sing in a beautiful voice while rest of the passengers listened:

> Reymundo: *Bum bompa, bum bompa, bum bompa, bum bompa*
> Luis: "*De la sierra morena,*
> *Cielito lindo, vienen bajando*
> *Un par de ojitos negros*
> *Cielito lindo, de contrabando.*
> *Ese lunar que tienes,*
> *Cielito lindo, junto a la boca,*
> *No se los des a nadie*
> *Cielito lindo, que a mi me toca.*"

Then the entire load of passengers joined in the chorus, in unison, some in high tones, others in a lower octave as they swung together from side to side.

> "*Ay, ay, ay, ay, canta y no llores*
> *Por que cantando se alegran*
> *Cielito lindo los corazones...*"

An angry Jack sat in the front, upset that his insult had backfired. Sergeant Rob laughed and said to him, "Lighten up, Jack, they got you pretty good this time. Let them have this one." Rob then proceeded to join in the chorus: "*Ay, ay, ay, ay, I am the man of Dolores!*" The van headed off into the desert landscape and slowly disappeared, but the laughter and the singing – "*Ay, ay, ay, ay, canta y no llores, por que cantando se alegran, cielito lindo, los corazones*" – could still be heard as the truck vanished over a hill.

Psyko, who dismissed it as silly, shook his head at Pretty Boy, who had gotten into the moment and joined in. Psyko waved his fingers as if to say, "You're dismissed." Pretty Boy sang at the top of his lungs, enjoying a rare moment of pure harmony.

Jack Gutierrez sat angrily looking out the window; he could not stand that the Sarge was not as upset with these animals as he was. Sergeant Rob turned the radio to a San Diego station. The DJ introduced the next song: "…and from the film *The Fabulous Baker Boys*, here's 'Jack's Theme' on San Diego's Jazz Eighty-Eight Point Three."
"Hey, Jack, they're playing your song," said Sergeant Rob jokingly, trying to shake off his partner's chronic misery. Sergeant Rob turned up the radio; Jack didn't respond. The sad tune made him reflect; he thought about his job, his anger, his lack of patience. He was miserable, but could not understand why. He became nostalgic; he thought about his days of innocence, happier times in his youth.

Jack was the eldest of five children born to Mexican parents who came to the United States legally in the late '50s. Neither of his parents spoke English. His father was an auto mechanic with a gambling problem, his mother a devoted wife and parent. They bought a little house in El Paso, Texas, across from Cuidad Juarez, Mexico, where Jack had been born. Jack became a U.S. citizen at 10 years old with his mother. He was a good-looking, dark-skinned kid. He had dimples when he smiled.

His younger siblings were all U.S. citizens. He began to grow resentful towards non-English speakers at an early age, and he adapted to the American culture and discouraged his younger brothers and sisters from speaking Spanish. He loved his parents but did not want them pushing the Spanish language on him and the other children. He wanted to be like the rest of the American kids.

He was a good student, a good kid and an excellent athlete; he played sports in high school. He got along well with everyone except kids who did not speak English. He didn't want himself or his siblings to have anything to do with them. His good-natured siblings eventually ignored him, leaving him embittered in his late teens. He loved American women but had high expectations of a partner for himself; he wanted the perfect woman, which eventually caused him to miss out on a lot of romantic opportunities. After graduating from community college, he had a series of supervisor jobs before joining the Border Patrol in the late 1980s. He wanted to find a woman and start a family, but his lack of skill in socializing with the opposite sex hindered him.

When he was 18 years old, his father gave him a 1968 Chevrolet Camaro upon his graduation; Jack was the first one in his family to graduate from high school. His father had bought the old used car chassis at a junk yard, put a new engine in it, painted it and presented it to him. Jack was on top of the world. Thirty days later, his father borrowed the car, supposedly to take it on a preventive maintenance drive. He returned home the next day walking. He'd lost the car in a card game.

In his late 30s, desperate and lonely, Jack married the first woman who took interest in him. She was an undocumented alien. He'd met her in a greasy spoon saloon grille; she was a waitress, and he asked her out. He remembered their first date, dancing the night away; she was chipping away at his hate for his own kind. The song "Mambo Italiano" by Cow Bop was playing. He was laughing and singing it to her as they swung and danced. He changed the lyrics to "Mambo Mexicano" and improvised the lyrics as she laughed.

The marriage quickly soured; it did not end well. They were married for five years and had a son; they named him John Tyler Gutierrez. Jack regressed to his angry self, and after five years of domestic violence and verbal abuse, she left after receiving her citizenship. She took her son and went to live with her brother in Colorado, where she eventually remarried. Jack began to gain weight, went into a depression, and was diagnosed with diabetes at 41 years old.

Pretty Boy

Bonifacio Segoviano Manzanero, AKA Pretty Boy, a good-looking,
fair-skinned young man, was the best green thumb in the Emerald
Triangle. He could clone and graft the Chronic to the Northern
Lights and have a summer harvest before the helicopters could find
their way towards his acreage. He always reeked of the kind (high
grade marijuana), which made him very popular among smokers, the
likes of Psyko or his associates. He had been deported so many times
he had lost track. Of course, mass consumption of cannabis sativa
didn't help his memory problem any. His was the proverbial rotating
door.

He had big sponsors who cultivated his talents as well as he
cultivated the Marijuana seedling. He was truly in high demand,
which made him cocky and shallow, but mostly vain. Pretty Boy
claimed he purposely had himself deported because he needed to go
to Mexico and his bosses down south needed reports from him.

Pretty Boy had a secret nobody knew. He was born in the U.S. but
had spent his summers in Sinaloa, Mexico, where he learned the
trade. He was an American citizen. He pretended to be illegal due to
his nefarious activities. His high-powered connections had scrubbed
his files from every available U.S. database. His father was an auto
body man who'd worked on buses in Sinaloa prior to legally
immigrating to America in 1990; Pretty Boy was born the following
year, in San Diego.

He claimed to be connected with the cartels, but nobody ever
believed him. He was constantly throwing out names of cartel
members who had been recently arrested or who'd been in the local
papers.

"I had a house in Gualala overlooking the Pacific; just me and four
of my workers," he told the other passengers on the van. "We would
set up camp in the hills of the state park before the planting season
and haul four full-size trucks filled with equipment, supplies, water

pumps, tubing, tents, sleeping bags, flashlights, spotlights, tree climbing gear…" You could have written a book called *Illegal Marijuana Cultivation In Large Scale On Uncle Sam's Dime* just by listening to this guy ramble on. "…seeds, tubs. Booby traps, plastic sheeting, walkie talkie radios, MREs (meals ready to eat), more food, portable TVs, AM/FM radio, lightweight camouflage netting, a 1,000-foot roll of drip irrigation hosing, and a couple of purebred pit bulls that act as additional security: Zeus and Hera. I named them after the two most powerful Greek Gods," he finished. "Oh, you're so smart because you know Greek mythology," quipped Nelly.

Pretty Boy really did know his business. He'd been raised planting illegal product in the hills of Sinaloa. His uncles and cousins all cultivated the little lamb tails, as the plant was called there; they never smoked it or harvested it, they only planted and moved on. Some other crew was responsible between the growing periods, and another crew did the harvesting. The different crews did not know each other; they reported to the general contractor, who issued contracts given out by the *jefe* controlling the area, usually the head of the most vicious narco family that had survived the local area's latest turf war. They'd perfected the blueprint from Sinaloa and simply transferred the entire process up north, like any powerful corporation moving its business to another country.

Telling his story, Pretty Boy remembered. He was on the phone: "Yeah, uh huh, okay, you sure though, no helicopters? All righty, green light it is, *ese*, *luz* effin *verde*, hell yeah. Let's get to work!" Four trucks drove up a rocky terrain surrounded by miles and miles of greenery. The men unloaded the trucks and organized the equipment and supplies in a systematic process, mostly by order of use.

Zeus, a large male pit bull terrier, a magnificent and muscular beast, was set free to roam as he pleased. He would signal with a bark if he sensed anyone approaching. Pretty Boy secretly prayed that Zeus wouldn't return with a bloody arm in his jaws. The idea crossed his mind; he imagined it, and then shook off the idea, uff! But Zeus mostly stuck to tormenting the rabbits, squirrels, lizards, and any moving creature that was not a human. Even a shackled and chained Hera got nipped by the alpha male. Pretty Boy claimed to have paid two thousand dollars for the purebred dog. Hera he got for a bargain price of eight hundred dollars.

Hera was chained to a tree. She was hot and miserable, she was muzzled. One of the workers signaled to Pretty Boy that he should give her water and food. Pretty Boy pretended to look at his watch and shook his head while signaling "not yet" with his index finger, one hand on his waist while he gyrated his mid-section; the dog had not had water or food in two days.

The area to be planted was marked; it was about ten acres near a known underground spring which Pretty Boy had hid last summer. The men began about the business of planting. Garden tools hit the dirt, a series of holes were dug straight as an arrow, row after row, two feet apart, in a giant square. Black drip irrigation was buried along the rows two inches deep. Prepared seedlings were carefully transplanted from tiny square containers. Pretty Boy talked to the baby plants as if they were his own offspring on their first day of school. The entire field was ready, but it needed water and camouflage to keep the nosy birds of the sky away. Time was of the essence. They need lots of water, now. They needed to locate the spring before the seedlings died off, buts it was too late to start looking and too dark; they waited until first light.

Back at camp, one man was frying up SPAM, tossing it onto a hot pan on the portable camping stove. Another was serving drinks, a third worker was putting away supplies, and a fourth guy was checking the vehicles. Everyone had a job. Pretty Boy started a crazy session of what he called the "Funky Pretty Boy Dance Hour." Zeus barked once. Pretty Boy put a cassette into his cassette player. The music began. It was "Insane in the Membrane" by Cypress Hill; he looked Zeus right in the eyes and said, "Who you trying to get crazy with, *ese*? Don't you know I'm loony?" Zeus tilted his head and looked at Pretty Boy with wonderment. Pretty Boy started to dance some crazy dances to the amusement of his workers. Then he started free styling from the top of the dome (off the cuff):

"Pretty Boy, uh, won't you plant your seed, all them
little hynas wanna do the deed
Do it to the left, do to the right, drink some honey
mead, smoke a little weed
Pretty Boy's flavor in the six one nine, do yourself a
favor, do the sixty nine
Gonna procreate, all the homies hate, cause all the
shorty in your hood got they period late
Uh uh uh, yea, Pretty Boy uh, in the Four Two oh my
G-O-D is the place to be uh Pretty Boy uh uh uh
Black and white scoping just a couple tards
Got my fake ass papers, but no papers to roll;
Zip me like a tied up hog, take me for a stroll,
Pretty Boy uh clone some Northern Lights,
give me some of that get me higher than a kite, uh
And please don't tell me that you got some Mañana,
it don't really matter, I just need some marijuana.
Uh uh uh, yea, Pretty Boy uh, in the Four Two oh my
G-O-D is the place to be uh Pretty Boy uh uh uh
Pretty Boy busted, jail bars rusted, overrun the
precinct worse than General Custer
Calling all cars with a code eleven, bust them in they
heads like I think I'm Phil Nevin
Raven, Mavin, head all shaven, scootin out the door,
with my fake gun waving
Pretty Boy uh, won't you smoke me out, people who
don't blaze, they all missing out
Uh uh uh, yea, Pretty Boy uh, in the Four Two oh my
G-O-D is the place to be uh Pretty Boy uh uh uh
Yea baby, Pretty Boy in da house, yea uh uh uh, yea,
Pretty Boy getting ya'll real high yea, yea, yea, yea,
and you don't stop, hell yea..."

The next morning Pretty Boy untied Hera who was dehydrated and had been in the same spot for three days. He put her on a leash. He took her for a walk near the field. He knelt down and talked to her, gave her a kiss, removed the muzzle and released her. She darted away and disappeared over a giant rocky area. The workers looked at each other, confused. Pretty Boy grabbed Zeus, who was now on a harness and leash. Pretty Boy gave him a command. Zeus immediately began to pull Pretty Boy over the rocks, down by an area full of high grass; within fifteen minutes he came across Hera, who was lapping up gallons of water from a muddy puddle. Pretty Boy stopped a hand-held stop watch, looked at it and said, "A new record, guys." He was so proud of his pets. He hugged them and began another series of crazy dances.

The men dug up the underground spring, connected a water pump to a solar-powered generator, then connected hundreds of feet of green tubing to the water pump. The green tubing zigzagged here and there, over the rocks and into the field where the drip irrigation hose stuck out of the ground. Pretty Boy used his walkie talkie radio to give the order, "Fire!" He watched the tubing, and after about two minutes a steady stream of fresh mountain water shot out. "Eureka!" yelled Pretty Boy. He connected the tubing to the drip irrigation hoses. Pretty Boy did another series of crazy dances; the workers looked at each other and cracked up, then tried unsuccessfully to imitate Pretty Boy. The job was done, for the moment.

The following week Pretty Boy was driving down Main Street, his plantation was now in the hands of another crew. He was about to regroup two of his workers; one had decided to go east where many workers were heading, to the Bakken Shale oil boomtowns of North Dakota. Pretty Boy was heading into a predominately Hispanic neighborhood when he came to a checkpoint. He wasn't worried since he had his driver's license and registration. When he saw the green Border Patrol trucks he put the palm of his hand on his forehead and muttered, "Aw, shit, not today." He wasn't expecting the INS. He stuck his license in the rubber plastic seam of the stick shift, where it fell through to the pavement.

The immigration officers, unable to prove his citizenship, loaded Pretty Boy on the van for deportation. They had a full van and were going to drive the passengers to a detention center in southeastern California for processing.

All these things Pretty Boy related as he gazed off into the distant landscape, it was as if talking about it was therapy for him. Reymundo spoke to all of them. He said, "You all are the People of the Sun. Lift your heads, have dignity. God has put you here for a reason; have you ever wondered why the almighty has put you here."

Psyko interrupted with a degrading laugh. "Yeah, maybe we had to sit through some more of your Aztec History class 'cause we're not Mexican enough, yea that must be it, old man!"

Reymundo put his head down, trying to understand why this young man had so much anger even when faced with doom. Luis responded, "I like your stories. I feel like I'm lifted up, like I'm worthy of respect like the warriors you talk about."

Pretty Boy and Psyko laughed. "Yeah, right, you're a warrior, but instead of riding the horse, the horse rides you!" The two laughed. "Naw man, seriously, tell us some more. Right, Psyko? It's pretty cool, man, we want to hear some more. You know any Greek mythology?" asked Pretty Boy.

"Don't get him started. Go on, old man, tell us more *Azteca Historia*," Psyko said sarcastically. Psyko really liked the stories Reymundo was telling, he just couldn't show anyone that he was human and had interests. "Okay, okay," said Reymundo.

The Rise and Fall of Aztatlan IV – The Supreme Warrior Nation

Now to the south was a land where the warriors of the Culhuacan lived. They were in a constant battle with their western neighbors, the Chalca. The Culhuacans made a pact with the new arriving band of warriors, the Mexica, that they would fight together against the Chalcas, which outnumbered both the Culhuacan and the Mexica. The Culhuacan chief promised the Mexica many tributes because he knew they were the fiercest warriors descending from the Chicomoztoca.

The Mexica sent two envoys, Tenoch and Ixtli Cualli; they were welcomed by the chief of the Culhuacan himself. When the chief saw Ixtli Cualli, he knelt before him as did the chief's entourage. They spoke to him and adored him. Ixtli Cualli was revered as a god. Now Tenoch, who was 15 years old by this time, did not care very much for things of that nature. Tenoch was more concerned for his people, as his father had taught him, than he was for being served or treated as royalty.

Tenoch was a true warrior, and this was a means to an end. A relationship with the Culhuacan would surely mean many battles that he would be involved in, and there was constant battle at that time. The envoys were treated well at the tribal village of the Culhuacan. The plans were laid for the invasion and the subsequent elimination of the Chalca.

Tenoch spoke to the chief of the Culhuacan. "My father, the chief elder and leader of his people, the Mexica, has given me full authority to speak for him. I ask but one thing in return for our allegiance and support in your wars with the Chalca tribe, which has done nothing to my people. I ask that you spare them and keep their society intact after we conquer their warriors. This I ask since we are in need of captives, many, many, captives. We do not wish to eliminate the Chalca, only to capture their fiercest warriors."

The chief of the Culhuacan spoke. "It is granted. Of what concern is it to me that you kill or capture the warriors of our enemy, as long as our enemy no longer poses a threat or competes with us for land, food, or hunt? However, I do ask that you allow your own cousin to stay with us here, for he is of remarkable stature and perfection. We will honor him with all privileges due unto him." Tenoch agreed.

They made the pact; they drank the boiled leaves of the tobacco, and also smoked some as well. They ate and were treated as fairly as any warrior could be treated. They planned and retreated each to their village or camp. When Tenoch arrived at his father's camp, he was questioned about his cousin. Tenoch explained that by mutual understanding, Ixtli Cualli would be the guest of the Culhuacan for an extended period. Ixtli Cualli seemed to prefer his ambassador status, and it was good for the Mexica to have somebody on the inside.

The chiefs and the elders of the Mexica met again. This time not only did Tenoch get invited, but he was the spokesperson, taking his role as a new leader supported by his father, who had full trust in the boy, who was now a man. "We will be allowed to capture as many Chalca as we want. We will fulfill our covenant with our Sun God Huitzlilopochtli by sacrificing the fiercest of the Chalca warriors. Let us inventory our weaponry and see where we fall short. Let us strategize on the manner of advancing so that we may have the advantage."

They pierced their earlobes with the needles of the maguey multiple times; they gathered the blood which was offered to the Sun God for a successful war. Only the elite – the upper commanding officers, the warrior chiefs – were allowed this privilege of bloodletting.

The next morning the warriors of the Mexica waited in the Valley of the Rain God Tlaloc, the God of the Culhuacan and the people of the surrounding areas. They were met by the warriors of the Culhuacan; there were about twelve thousand warriors in all. They marched on, some with spears and *macuahuitle* (wooden clubs with sharp obsidian pieces lodged in them), others had *hachas* (axes), and many had slings. They crossed into Chalca territory in the midmorning, before the Sun God had made his peak.

They heard the Chalca before they saw them, and when they finally saw them it was as a cloud of dust kicking up high into the sky. Twenty thousand Chalcas approached an oncoming Mexica/Culhuacan army. The Chalcas, in a frenzy under the spell of the mushroom, screamed and advanced on the enemy, who waited patiently. Tenoch gave the order to attack, but reminded the warriors that the mightiest of the Chalcas were to be taken alive.

Tenoch waited for the screaming, approaching front line to get within fifty feet, then gave the order to the bowmen who shot poisoned arrows behind the oncoming slew of Chalcas, isolating the first group. It was a genius plan because it separated the large mass into parts that could easily be dealt with.

Outnumbered and outweaponed by an enemy in a haze of fury, the Mexica successfully outmaneuvered their enemies. The Culhuacan watched in amazement at the efficiency that the warriors of the raggedy tribe displayed. Such bravery had never been witnessed. One Mexica warrior could take down two Chalcas with one swift blow of his *macuahuitle*, while two assistants would bind the feet and hands of the enemy. The Mexica quickly had many Chalca warriors bound and hogtied under the hot sun. They were constantly watching each other's backs. The Chalca tribe was finally conquered but not eliminated.

Two days the battle raged and for two days the Chalcas were captured by the Mexica. The Culhuacan, now reduced to spectators, witnessed what was to become the future of warfare. After establishing that the Chalcas were now inferior to the new nation of the Culhuacan and Mexica people, the chief of the Culhuacan was so pleased he offered his daughter, Princess Xochityl, to the Mexica leader, young Tenoch, who had led the capture of over three hundred Chalca warriors and the killing of hundreds more. Tenoch had swooped down like an eagle upon its prey, with the strength of a jaguar. He did it all in the name of the Sun God Huitzilopochtli.

When Tenoch saw Princess Xochityl, he was struck as if with a bolt of lightning. He knelt on one knee and lowered his head in submission. Her beauty surpassed that of any woman he had ever seen. She was a true beauty to behold. Now when Tenoch, the jaguar hunter, learned of her being given to him, he set about conquering her heart.

They became enamored with each other, and she was to become the new princess of the Mexica. Mexitli, the chief of all the Mexica, announced the preparation for the sacrificial ceremonies to take place. They built temporary wooden altars that they would use to sacrifice thousands of warriors over the next month. The stage had been set for what was to become the practice for the next few hundred years.

Food was brought by many surrounding tribes paying tribute to the new warrior nation of Mexica; tribes came from afar to witness the covenants to the Sun God Huitzilopochtli and the Water God Tlaloc. They brought baskets of grain, *maize*, berries, peppers, squash, *tomatl*, and nopal, along with many other common foods.

Ceremonial dances took place all day long. The first sacrificial victim was cleansed by the women and brought by the warriors into the main plaza. His face was painted black and his body was adorned with precious stones. He was tied to a large stone and given a wooden knife.

The warriors danced around him with knives and poked him as he slowly bled. He was taken up to the altar and held by his feet and hands. The Mexica priest, brother of Mexitli, raised his obsidian razor-edged knife and plunged it into the chest of the mighty warrior, who let out a scream. The priest stuck his hand into the opening of the chest cavity and removed the still-beating heart, raised it to the heavens in the name of the Sun God Huitzilopochtli, and threw it into an elaborately decorated wooden bowl.

The body was given to an awaiting priest who cut off the legs, the arms and the head and threw the torso to yet another set of priests. Each part of the body was given to a selected member of the ruling elite. The next victim, in order of bravery on the battlefield, was brought up. This sacrificing and removing of the heart continued throughout the day and into the night. Almost three hundred Chalca warriors were sacrificed on the first day alone.

The wooden altar was red with blood, as was a thirty-foot diameter perimeter, and all those involved were painted in red as they danced around ceremoniously. Conch shells sounded day and night, and the parts of the bodies were given out and boiled into soups of *maize*, peppers, and *tomatl*; this was the original *pozole*. The skulls were cracked open like coconuts, the brains extracted and consumed. The heads were placed on spikes around the entire encampment; it was a horrific sight.

The remaining twenty-nine days consisted of the same rituals until all of the Chalca warriors were scarified to appease the Sun God. The word of the Mexica spread throughout the nation. All the tribes were on alert. The Culhuacan were horrified but intrigued and followed the Mexica's example. The blood created a new covenant with the gods; both tribes had now adopted the god of their enemy, the Rain God Tlaloc. The consuming of the flesh and brains, and the drinking of the blood, gave the transfer of power to those who consumed it in the name of the gods. The greater the warrior whose flesh was consumed, the greater the power inherited.

"Man, I would love to be there fighting alongside my brothers. I would kill those Chalcas, man, I would be all chewing *peyote* and drinking *pulque* and fighting and they would serve me.... Man, why couldn't I have been born at that time?" cried out Pretty Boy.

"We are born when we are born. I hope you all understand why you are so deep, why your thirst for blood and revenge is so strong. Your talents and your person have been suppressed for five hundred years. Take note, young Aztatlanteans. Make your marks," Reymundo said.

The Housekeeper

Nelly was telling Luis about her favorite food, *carne asada* fries. She asked him if he had ever had them. Psyko interrupted, "Yeah, I think Ranas would rather have some horse cock!" Pretty Boy almost died of laughter.

Doña Rosa repeated what he had said, nodding her head as if she understood what they were saying. "Horse Coke, jes!" she exclaimed, excited to be part of the conversation. Psyko turned angrily towards her and said, "Bitch, you don't know what I'm saying. You want some horse cock?"

"Jes, jes, horse Coke!" she repeated, proud of herself for being part of the English-speaking crowd incorrectly assuming that they were referring to the soft drink.

Pretty Boy was dying of laughter as Psyko prodded the poor old woman, who was only repeating and nodding like she did every day in the English-speaking world. "You want some horse cock in you, in your mouth?" Psyko asked as he made hand gestures with his hand to his mouth. "Jes, jes, good, good!" Responded the poor woman still believing it was all casual conversation.

This made Pretty Boy fall to the floor of the van, wriggling and holding his stomach as Psyko made a fool of the old woman with the chubby cheeks and a bad case of pockmarks riddling her face. "You guys are freegin assholes! Leave her alone, *cholo*. Quit making fun of her!" yelled Nelly at both of them.

"How the hell does somebody spend ten years in the U.S. and not learn one damned word of English?" Psyko barked towards Nelly, as if he were better off because he spoke English or at least some ghetto variation.

Doña Rosa wanted so badly to have been part of the American Dream, but holding two jobs while raising her three kids hadn't allowed her to attend the free English classes that were held nightly at the recreation center. Fortunately for Doña Rosa, she was oblivious to any insult thrown her way. She thought they were laughing with her. She began talking to the young Salvadoran seated beside her as if she were schooling him on aspects of American life.

Yeyo, the young Salvadoran, had been in the United States barely two months before he was deported. He figured that all these English-speaking big shots could teach him a thing or two about the language, and maybe next time he could stay in the U.S. longer. He listened intently to the din of chatter among the crowd. His eyes were especially fixed on Doña Rosa, whom he figured was the wisest of all.

"Yo trabajaba en una empresa que fabricaba turbinas de aviones en Rockford, alla en Illinois. Yo entraba y salia en lugares de la planta en donde uno nesesita accesso militar, yo estaba encargada de limpeza and los banos y oficinas. No a qualquiera le dan accseso alli tienes que pasar una serie de..." Doña Rosa was chatting away to Yeyo.

"What's she telling him, Ranas?" Nelly asked Luis, since her grasp of Spanish was limited to ordering carne asada fries at the Aztlan Taco & Muffler Shop. It was called that because it was a taco shop in the front and the owners brother had set up a quick and dirty muffler shop out back in the rear of the small building. The hand painted "Muffler" sign for the shop included some hand scribbled text somebody had added later, with a black marker, that always cracked Nelly up: "No Muff Too Tuff."

Luis translated for Nelly "she's telling him that she worked at a company in Rockford, Illinois, that manufactures aerospace components. And that she had high security clearance throughout the whole plant, because she was an employee of a janitorial service contractor. Many workers were blocked from accessing these sensitive areas that she spent nights walking through. She saw tons of blueprints but didn't know what they were for. The engineers were very nice to her and everyone liked her." Doña Rosa was one of thousands of undocumented workers with access to sensitive sites hired by less than respectable companies that sidestepped the E-Verify hiring process for government workers by hiring illegal aliens with fake ID cards. The government didn't care as long as the service contractor had passed the vetting process.

Doña Rosa continued to tell Yeyo about the night she was caught by La Migra (INS). *"Es que yo le habia dicho, a mi esposo, que estaba cansada de que tomaba tanto con sus amigos, tarbajaba todo el dia y en su tiempo libre con ellos mientras yo me quedo sola con los chamacos...."*

Luis began translating for Nelly. "She says she was telling her husband that she was tired of being left alone with the kids while he went out drinking with his buddies during his time off from his busy work schedule. So he promised her that they would go out on Thursday night to the local club, Palenque." Thursday night was karaoke night, and she used to love listening to him belt out *boleros* like in the old days, when he had first won her heart. He was the most handsome man in the world, and owned her heart. He was very hard working and loved his kids, and she loved him to death. The only problem was that he loved drinking with his buddies.

Doña Rosa continued to tell her story in Spanish. She had met her husband in Mexico and they were married after knowing each other a month; she was crazy about him. She was a short, curvy, sexy lady, and he liked her moves; they met in a club in Guadalajara. He was six foot two inches tall, ruggedly handsome, and enjoyed her easy demeanor. He won her heart by singing *boleros* to her on the karaoke. He had a wonderful voice, and she loved it when he would sing to her. They crossed into the United States together ten years and, as she says, fifty pounds ago.

Once they arrived in the U.S., they both found jobs. She cleaned houses and office buildings; he worked in a produce market loading trucks. On Thursday nights they would go to a local club, which they found, for karaoke night; he would sing *boleros* to the delight of the crowd. She'd loved those times, the good old days. She always requested that he sing her favorite song, *"En Mi Viejo San Juan,"* because it reminded her of her town on the outskirts of Guadalajara: San Juan, Jalisco, Mexico. The rest of the women in the club were envious of her and she felt like a queen.

Their three boys were born U.S. citizens, which was their goal; the first came two years after their arrival. The Thursday night dates to the Palenque karaoke night became less and less frequent. He recently told her that they would spark their romance once again. He told her to leave the kids with the neighbor, get dressed, and meet him at the laundromat downtown at 7 p.m.; he would pick her up right after work. She was there at 6:45; the immigration officers picked her up at 6:50. She was so sad for her husband, who was left alone without knowledge of her whereabouts. She was a ghost now; she would become a memory to her children, and if she didn't get back across, they would eventually forget her.

She was taken to a detention facility, fingerprinted, and held for two days before they loaded her into a bus en route to Arizona. She picked a seat towards the back, where she felt more comfortable. She sat next to a young man. They introduced themselves; her name was Rosa, and he was Yeyo.

Her story, told to the other passengers on the bus, ended there. What Rosa never knew was that her husband had set her up. She never realized that a few years after his debut in the karaoke bar, her husband was approached after one of his performances at the club by a temptress, a good looking older lady with money, a woman who had never been married and got her thrills bedding married men; it was her revenge against men for the years of abuse and torment she had endured at their hands. Her name was Vanessa Delgado. She was smitten by the tough but handsome tall man with the short wife. She'd approached him and handed him her business card. She promised him stardom and success with no strings attached. It was true there weren't any strings; they were more like wire rope.

Rosa's husband decided to give the spinster a call from the warehouse pay phone at his job. They agreed to meet; she would pick him up at lunch the next day. She arrived promptly outside the warehouse when all the men were going to lunch. She pulled up in a fancy black European sports car and picked him up like a male prostitute on Sunset Boulevard. She proceeded to take him to lunch at a fancy restaurant. She opened up a new world to him, a world that he otherwise would never have known.

She talked him into calling in sick the rest of the day, and she took him to a motel where they consummated their new love. He was reeled in, hook, line, and sinker. They managed to keep their affair secret for years. Vanessa, however, was too attached to the man with the golden voice and vowed to herself that she would destroy him if he ever left her.

She came up with a plan for how they could be together. She played it out for him one night and it sure sounded foolproof; his only problem was how he would get over the guilt he would feel for the woman he was about to betray.

Vanessa had connections with police, lawyers and more importantly, the Immigration and Naturalization Service. She would guarantee him full citizenship, but he would have to betray his wife. Vanessa convinced Rosa's husband to lure his wife to a location at a certain time.

After she showed up, immigration officers would pick her up and deport her. Rosa would no longer pose a threat to the professional lady with the devious plans. Vanessa convinced him that he would feel guilty for a very short time, but with her support, he would get over it very soon. They would be together and she would raise his boys as if they were her own. He bought was she was selling, the whole package.

When the illegals arrived at the Arizona transfer center, they were loaded into Border Patrol vans. Rosa and Yeyo were the last two to get off the bus, and all the Border Patrol vans were full. They would have to wait until the next day. "We have a special trip going to San Diego. You can load these two in here," yelled Sergeant Rob to the Border Patrol coordinator in charge of assigning deportees to all trucks heading toward the Ports of Exit.

"OK, that will save me a lot of work," responded the coordinator. Psyko, with something on his mind, interrupted the conversation and said, "I write music too. Your girly friend, Ranas, ain't the only one with talent. I wrote a song right now." He looked towards Pretty Boy and said, "Pretty Boy, lay down a beat gee!" Pretty Boy immediately went into his beat box mode and was surprisingly good.

> *"The two one three will put a bullet in your scrotum, rolling through desert makes my shit all distorted, cuz.*
>
> *I'm traveling through the west, Bonifacio dropping rhymes, these are the stories of the dearly deported, yea yea yea dearly deported yea yea,.*
>
> *These are the stories, these are the stories, these are the stories of the dearly deported yea yea yea,.*

As Pretty Boy continued making beat box sounds, Psyko went on:

> *"In my hood I'm a legend, the truth I don't be stretchin, ask a girl to make a sandwich, in a jiffy she'll be fetchin.*
>
> *Seeing saddened faces, filling empty spaces, People sitting here from all different places cuz.*

*They're coming from the eight one eight and the two
one three, they're wishing they had papers; yea we'd
all be free.*

*But life ain't easy, no, not one bit, If you ain't got no
real papers they treat you all like shit, cuz,*

*I'm travelin with no dope. All my shit got snorted,
and these are the stories of the dearly deported, yea
yea yea.*

*These are the stories, these are the stories, these are
the stories of the dearly deported yea yea yea.*

Psyko gave Pretty Boy a fist bump and sat back as if he had proven
he was as slick and cultured as the rest of them.

"That was pretty good, young Chicano!" Reymundo praised.
"Yeah, that wasn't bad," Nelly interjected as if she wasn't
thoroughly impressed. She couldn't admit that Psyko was growing
on her. All these years she'd avoided his type, but now that she was
face to face with a thug like Psyko, she saw that he was just as
human as she was.

Lunch Stop – Jack's Pudding

As the people began to stumble out of the van towards the shade, Jack barked orders like a Marine sergeant. "Stay in one single file, you understand a damned single file?" He screamed, "Of course you don't, you dumb animals, that's why you got your asses caught and are now the property of Jack Gutierrez, Customs and Border Patrol Agent Extraordinaire!" Psyko was the third one out and started to walk. As if to defy his captors, he strutted like a pimp with his hands raised in the air as he performed a Crip walk and free-styled a flow of rap, ridiculing the tyrant.

> *"South-Siders coming down your street creepy creep, creepy crawl, we're always packing heat, creepy creep, sagging draws,*
>
> *Representing the two one three can't you understand;*
>
> *We're sling slanging, big booty banging, left yo mama begging for some moe butt slammin;*
>
> *Top-o-da-dome, I can see you just don't contemplate, Officer Jack, stroking his club, gonna masterbate;*
>
> *Yeeuh yeeuh, haw haw haw; que no cabrones, bajense los chones, ponte a trabajar pinche bola de huevones;*
>
> *La Nelly Fria, es una cremilla, pero ella bien sabe que le urge una cojida*
>
> *Si ya sabritas... pues pa que barcel getting out of jail, Bonifacio, cloning, muda-effin holy grail...!"*

Kapow! Psyko got hit upside the back of his neck and upper back area with Jack Gutierrez's billy club and fell to the ground like a slaughterhouse heifer. The women screamed and covered their mouths. Sergeant Rob quickly stopped Jack Gutierrez from striking a second blow while Psyko laid in a twisting, writhing mass.

"Jesus Jack, what the hell, man?" Rob yelled in disgust. "You know what kind of shit you're going to get me into, pulling this shit again? You want me to face the board again? Son of a bitch, Jack!"

"Did ya see the way he was mocking us? God knows what he was planning, some kind of a gang call. Sergeant, I'm looking out for you and me, man, I don't want this piece of shit disrespecting us!" retorted Jack.

"Who the hell is he going to call, Jack? We're in the middle of the damned desert, there ain't nobody around for miles. Who's he gonna call, Jack? A goddamn California Condor? You think his homeboy is gonna jump out a muther freegin saguaro and pop a cap in your ass, Jack? Eff me, shit, disrespect us? You're sounding like him, Jack. Help me get him up and back into the van. Son of a bitch!" Sergeant Rob knew this scenario all too well. He had spent the better part of the last decade covering for his partner.

"You're freegin going soft, Sarge. You know how these beaners are. They start with the gang signs and next thing you know we have a goddamn mutiny on the mother-freegin Bounty!" Jack insisted.

"They're freegin dehydrated, half-starved, scared and weak. What kind of a threat do they freegin pose, huh, Jack? Tell me."

"*Eres un pinche malinchista!*" cried out Doña Rosa.
"What's a maleta chispa what what?" whispered Pretty Boy to Reymundo.

"A *malinchista,* not a maleta chispa. A *malinchista* is a Mexican who betrays his own people, like the infamous Indian *La Malinche*. She sold out the Aztecs to the Spaniards, greatly hurrying their demise. People who betray Mexicans are referred to as *malinchista*," responded Reymundo, keeping his eyes on the activity in front of him with great fear and concern. This was no joy ride, and they were sacrificial lambs.

Sergeant Rob went inside the gas station and grabbed ice. He instructed Officer Jack to get premade sandwiches or burritos and Gatorade, fourteen servings, one for each, and a pudding pop or something. He handed Jack his debit card; Jack already knew the PIN. Officer Jack did as he was told. There were no pudding pops, so he grabbed twelve pudding cups instead, six chocolate and six tapioca, on his way out. Before he hit the door, he saw all the food that he was carrying. It killed him that Uncle Sam was spending good money on these people, who as far as he was concerned had already raped this country.

He opened the pudding cups halfway, and quickly began to slurp out half the contents while looking out for Sergeant Rob. He then applied the foil lids back into place. While halfway through the last chug, he looked over at the cashier, who was looking at him in disgust, and muttered, "Whiskey Tango Foxtrot, bro?"

Officer Jack distributed the lunches, drinks, and puddings, making a loud to-do so that Sergeant Rob, who was busy tending to Psyko, could hear him. The break was longer than expected due to the first aid situation. When Sergeant Rob was done with Psyko, he went up to Jack, who was chowing down on his second sandwich and drinking his second Gatorade. "Gimme his lunch," Rob said, motioning toward Psyko, who was sitting on a downed wooden telephone pole that was used as a property line divider. "I'm giving it to him. I want you to stay away from him, Jack, I'm serious." "There ain't no more," shrugged Jack with his mouth full as he stuffed half a sandwich into his mouth.

"Well, is there one for me at least?"

"Sure, boss, of course." He handed Rob a sandwich and drink. "Pudding?" asked the Sergeant. "Sorry, they ran out, Chief."

Sergeant Rob walked over to Psyko and handed him the lunch. Psyko eagerly ate and drank, the movement of his jaws causing a great pain in the back of his neck.

They loaded everyone back into the van. Sergeant Rob looked over at Jack and said, "Get your *maleenichista* ass in the cab," and shook his head. The van rolled on in the hot desert.

Nelly was not afraid of Psyko anymore, and feeling sorry for him, she began to make small talk, riddling him with questions. "Oakland Raiders, huh? Are you from Oakland?"

Psyko just smiled and said in a pained voice, "Uh-uh. I want to hear some more about the Azteca Nation."

"Certainly, young warrior, certainly," said an eager Reymundo.

The Rise and Fall of Aztatlan V – The Eagle, the Snake, and the Cactus

After the thirty day ceremony, Mexitli went out into the wilderness, consumed salvia, *peyotl*, and other hallucinogenics, and then prayed to the Sun God and prophesized. He had a remarkable vision. He saw himself near a large lake in a valley, and in the middle of the lake was a rock where the *nopal* cactus grew from the rock. He saw that around his feet he was surrounded by rattlesnakes, hundreds of them. He froze in his tracks; he was afraid.

Mexitli knew the bite of the rattlesnake was an agonizing pain. Then he heard his son screaming above. Mexitli looked up in the sky and saw Tenoch with the body of an eagle. The eagle with the face of Tenoch swooped down by Mexitli's feet and grabbed each and every snake that was around his father, then flew up high into the blue sky and dropped the reptiles, which fell to the ground, killing each one as it smashed to the earth. When Mexitli was safe, Tenoch grabbed the last snake with his powerful talons and flew towards the rock where the cactus grew in the middle of the lake. Then Tenoch, the eagle, ate the snake upon the rock. Mexitli knew that he would be safe in that place, and that he should set off to find this new promised land.

Mexitli spoke with his son Tenoch about his vision, and then they both sat down with the elders, the priests, and the warrior chiefs and discussed the meaning of this dream, the prophecy. They all agreed that the sacrifices pleased the Sun God and that the promised land was close at hand. The main elders and warrior chiefs went to the Culhuacan village where they spoke with their counterparts, who gave them safe voyage beyond the limits of the territories. The Culhuacan were glad to see this dominating class of warrior leave their lands because of their Godlike fierceness in war. The Culhuacan invited the chiefs of the Mexica for a ceremonial banquet and sacrifice.

When the Mexica arrived, they saw that Itxli Cualli was adorned in beautiful feathers and golden accessories. He was a sight to behold;

four of the most beautiful Culhuacan young women were his concubines. Ixtli Cualli was a God on earth. He spoke to the Mexica as if they were below him, as if they missed their opportunity to serve him. Itxli Cualli was waited on hand and foot. The women of the village drew straws to see who would have the honor of bathing him, dressing him, adoring him.

Warriors danced about and sang tributes to Ixtli Cualli, who listened to their beautiful songs describing his lineage directly from the divine seed. It was as if the entire tribe had found their long-lost God. An entourage of handsomely adorned beauties and young warrior men escorted Itxli Cualli to a newly erected golden throne. It was a wooden seat with hammered gold leaf mined from the Sierra Madre. A golden cup was laid on a golden table along with an obsidian knife with a golden handle.

The Mexica were in awe; they could not believe their eyes. Yes, they were happy for their kin, mostly because they now had somebody pulling strings on the inside. They watched as the Culhuacan priests made elaborate dances and then, after chewing on *peyotl* mixed with salvia, they passed around a pipe filled with tobacco.

Suddenly, six of the biggest Culhuacan warriors grabbed Ixtli Cualli and threw him onto the table. Two grabbed his feet and two grabbed his arms; the other two stood watch. The high priest took the golden handled obsidian knife and plunged it into the chest of Ixtli Cualli. Ixtli Cualli barely had a chance to let out a scream before he died. The high priest shoved his hand into the chest cavity and removed a beating heart.

The Mexica leaders could not believe their eyes; the Mexica warrior chiefs would have killed the Culhuacan if not for Mexitli holding them off. "We will respect their sacrifice as they have respected ours. You see, they have only done what we have showed them, but they have actually chosen the most perfect specimen who best embodies the Sun God. Ixtli Cualli has been given the highest honor a tribe can give to a man."

As Mexitli, the Mexica chief, spoke to his people, the Culhuacan high priest held the beating heart up to heaven and spoke. "Oh Sun God Huitzilopochtli, we honor you and feed your soul with this heart, which symbolizes a star. Just as the stars in the night would have vanquished you if not for this heart that we give to you as a food source, so you can now vanquish the stars and the night, and continue on to tomorrow!" The high priest spoke these things as the audience was in a state of disbelief and frenzy.

Reymundo finished his story as he looked at his fellow occupants. Everyone on the van listened intently to the unbelievable tales that were told as if Reymundo had witnessed them firsthand. Reymundo had a knack for telling a story in such detail that his audience wondered if he had some divine insight or some ancestral guidance that spoke to his soul.

Live from Phoenix with Marty Silvers

Back in Phoenix, Marty Silvers sat in a federal courthouse petitioning for a Moratorium of Deportation. An old bald man in a business suit sat beside him. The bags under Marty's eyes were a testament to his desperate attempt to stop Nelly's deportation. The last twenty-four hours had been a constant uphill battle of judicial letdowns, as well as a rollercoaster of emotions.

Marty had first met Nelly five years ago when she was 12 years old. He remembered the precocious little girl that wore glasses and a ponytail, peppering him with questions about law, life, and whatever else her obsessive little mind had selected as the topic for the day. He remembered being careful to give her the right answers but encouraging her to always, dig, dig, dig, until she could find the right answer herself.

He saw her grow into the beautiful young lady who now occupied his entire being. All these years he was secretly in love with the young lass, but her age kept him from allowing himself to let the subject even enter his mind. Now she was but a mere two weeks from her eighteenth birthday; she would be of legal age. But he was faced with the problem of keeping her from being torn from the country she knew and loved. Here was an opportunity to help her hugely. He would be in her favor forever and would be the man who had rescued her, her knight in shining armor. He felt guilty knowing that deep inside, it was a selfish thought. She deserved, by every right, to stay in this country. He had exhausted every avenue he could find. He had used all his resources, cal

led in all favors. His bank account had quickly dwindled away. Nothing mattered now but his success in what he thought was the most important case of his young life. At 29 years old, he had quickly risen through the ranks as a sharp public defender, and was now trying to make partner at a prestigious private law firm which had given him the green light to pursue this case pro bono.

He felt good. He knew that he would be able to face her and hug her, and she would know that he had gone through hell and high water. A door opened and his name and case file were called. "Mortimer Silvers, Fast Track, docket number 0612221." Marty stood up from his seat, as did the bald businessman sitting next to him. They shook hands and the man said to Marty, "We're even, bud. Got to go, call me with a verdict. Good luck." A restless looking older man spewed out some legal mumbo jumbo and then looked at Marty. "It appears your request has been approved."

Marty exhaled a big sigh of relief, the breath of a man who had been pardoned. He made a fist with his left hand and closed his eyes and looked up to thank God. This was his own personal battle with Goliath, and he had won. He was so proud of himself, his father would have been so proud of him, he couldn't wait to walk – no, run – to his car, to the....
"However."

Marty's heart sank. That "however" stuck him right where it hurt. It was not good to hear a "however," not now, anytime but now.

"However, it appears that your client is already being deported. San Diego, California, in to Tijuana, Mexico. I'm very sorry; there is nothing I can do at this time."
Marty ran to his car while calling his cousin Darlene on his cell phone. He told her he would drive to San Diego with the paperwork. She insisted on coming along, as did her friends. He drove like a mad man to pick them up.

He had a little black box in his glove compartment. It was a diamond engagement ring. He figured he could tell Nelly that they could get married and she could file for citizenship; a desperate plan for a desperate man. They raced to San Diego.

Marty arrived at his cousin's house, where she was waiting for him with Catalina. The girls got into the car and Marty told them how Nelly was already being deported and that his plan was to catch up to them and present the Border Patrol officers with his legal order to stop the deportation. It was already one in the afternoon, and he had no idea if they were still in the states or if the Border Patrol had already deported Nelly. He counted on the fact that government agencies were not the most efficient, and he hoped that they were behind schedule.

It was a long and grueling drive. He calculated that the Border Patrol vehicle had left at nine in the morning and that by the time Marty started his drive they were halfway there, approximately in Yuma, at the California border. His Mustang roared along Highway 8 heading west, arriving at Yuma in record time.

Marty figured that if he continued at the speed he was going, he would be able to catch them in the outskirts of San Diego. The drive from Phoenix to San Diego would normally take him about five and a half hours. A government vehicle carrying a full load of people would take about eight hours. He planned on making it in four; a goal that would save Nelly from getting deported, earn him a speeding ticket, or get them all killed.

Padre Mundo

Father Reymundo Ochoa Lopez Lopez, also known as Padre Mundo, was something of an enigma. It seemed he had done about as much bad as he had done good. He described his own soul as a perfect symbol of the yin and yang, an eternal poetic swirl of light and dark, good and evil, two constant opposing forces fighting for control of his soul. He was ordained a Catholic priest in 1989 and preached at a small church outside of Rosarito, Baja California, Mexico.

He had a great following even though he sometimes, or most times, employed some unorthodox methods to get his message across. He was becoming more well-known than the bishop of the diocese. The people loved him, which enraged the upper crust. They wanted so badly to get rid of the hard-working unorthodox rebel known for taking a little – no, a lot – more than necessary of the sacramental wine to be "full of the word of God," as he so often put it.

When the SARS epidemic hit, all the Mexican dioceses ordered their churches to stop all public gatherings that were not absolutely necessary, until further notice. Padre Mundo, however, continued to give the word of God to his sheep out in the communities and to those who couldn't come to the church. This he did much to the chagrin of his superiors. He even rejected a direct command from the Vatican to stop preaching and conducting Masses until the epidemic was over; he did not and went on with even more fervor.

Of course the letters to the Vatican were one-sided and the evidence against Padre Mundo was heavily piled on, if not grossly embellished. The episode divided the community so much that the Catholic Church threatened to excommunicate him.

Padre Mundo had always gone against the grain, a quality that allowed him to break the traditional barriers of the church but caused much grief to those who tried to control his actions. The padre continued to meet with community groups regarding many issues that the church had not approved; he was committed to helping the

community solve its issues of gang violence, domestic violence, lost youth, troubled marriages, and general poverty within the area.
He set up an unofficial school in a donated building. It wasn't much, but it gave the poorer children an opportunity to learn to read and write, and it gave them a place to hang around when their parents were busy working. He organized a group of volunteers and trained them to provide reading and writing assistance to anyone who showed up. It was a co-op of sorts and was the pride of the poor rural area which otherwise never would have experienced that type of guidance from the church.

The church leaders eventually convinced the authorities to bulldoze the illegal school, which had been erected in an area that in itself was a squatters' haven. All of the buildings in the area were illegal, but the government did not dare touch them for fear of causing a public outcry and a general working-man protest. The school, however, was authorized for razing since it wasn't actually a home that would have displaced a family.

Padre Mundo did not give up and continued to preach and meet with the community even after the church suspended him for failure to follow direct orders. Two days after the bulldozing incident, Padre Mundo received the worst news he could have imagined. His nephew, his sister's son, who had come from the south of Mexico to stay with him five years before, had been killed in an automobile accident on a local road. It was too much for the man of the cloth to handle, and with the pressure he was facing, he decided to re-evaluate his decisions.

He agreed to stop the nonsanctioned church gatherings the day that his beloved nephew Victor, only 19 years old, crashed head-on into a telephone pole. Padre Mundo was distraught. He was last seen leading a funeral procession through downtown Rosarito; it would be the last official rite he would perform for the church. As he slowly walked, tears rolled down his face while two rusty off-key trumpets played "*Las Golondrinas.*"

He was sent on a binational mission to the United States on a diplomatic visa with other friars. Once he was in the U.S. he sidestepped his colleagues, overstayed his visa and quit the church a broken man. He left his calling behind.

MacArthur Park

Reymundo sat on a bench in Los Angeles's MacArthur Park. It was 10 a.m.; he was sipping from a 20 ounce bottle of water which he had received as a handout. His hair was unkempt. He was wearing some dollar store reading glasses with the one of the ear guards pieced together with Scotch tape. A wholesale electronics store was playing the Tupac video for "California Love."

Transients dug for aluminum cans out of a trash can; another one harassed passing pedestrians for spare change. Menacing people stared at any newcomers, and a cotton candy seller was giving a child a tasty treat which his mother has just paid for after much pleading from the toddler. Across the street, at Panaderia Lupita's, a baker had just placed a freshly baked cake outside to cool. It was beginning to sprinkle. Reymundo was reading the jobs section of *La Opinion*.

"*Seccion de Trabajos... mecanico, ensamblador, mesero, niñera...* housekeeping, housekeeping, housekeeping, housekeeping, *chinga su Madre*, there's a lot of dirty houses in Los Angeles!" he muttered to himself. Most of the jobs were asking for papers. "I could do that," Reymundo said to himself in a low voice, then laughed in a low tone. He had a lot of spirit for a man who had lost it all, but when you had nothing left to lose, only then could you feel truly free.

The sound of a deep, rhythmic thump vibrated from a vehicle two blocks away. A 1971 grey primered Chevrolet Monte Carlo approached and dropped off a passenger. A 20-something-year-old in scraggily sweats with a shaved head and a white wife beater got out, looked both ways and then hurried into the park towards the tunnels; one hand was in his pants pocket. He walked by hurriedly, almost nervously, ignoring everyone but looking out for cops. "*Mota mota,*" a gruff-voiced older man signaled to the young man, who ignored him.

The young man was met inside the tunnel by two young scraggily men, then a third. It appeared that the young man gave them each a packet which he retrieved from his sweatpants pocket. The three young men each gave him a wad of cash, which he quickly counted. He chastised one of them for being short, then slapped him on the back of the head. He said something to them, then signaled with his finger to say he would be back later. He semi-jogged back to the vehicle, this time like a man with no worries, even with a bit of a smile. He jumped into the car, signaled to the driver – his finger like a gun shooting in the forward direction – and they sped away.

Every *conecta* at MacArthur Park worked this way. You had your field guys selling your product, then a supervisor who came around three or four times a day picking up the cash and replenishing supplies. There were the three guys who dealt the *chiva* – slang for heroin – then there were seven guys who sold *mota*, a steady and popular product even though it was mostly dirt weed full of seeds, sticks and stems.

There was no coke dealer at MacArthur Park; it was a rich man's game, and rich men didn't drive to the seedy part of town. If they were hurting for a fix they usually got it elsewhere. By far the most popular product at MacArthur Park was crystal meth. There were around fourteen meth dealers at any given time at the park. There was a high turnover rate among sellers; most dealers got high off their own supply and ended up sprung, addicted. Those were known as *crikosos*, and they were worthless to the supervisors. On any given a day a *crikoso* would disappear and was replaced by another dealer, quickly and without a hitch; a seamless process. There wasn't a high demand for crack, surprisingly. That was dealt in other areas of Los Angeles: downtown, South Central, and any and all black neighborhoods, for whatever reason.

Then there were the Green Card stores that surrounded the park. They were peppered between pizza joints, taco shops, *pollo asado* sellers, newspaper stands and other places of business where hundreds of people shopped, ate, and sometimes stole. These passport shops were the most lucrative ones. They pretended to sell passport photos or vehicle registration services but were actually fronts for fake I.D. cards, driver licenses, Green Cards, visas, passports, and even college degrees. If you needed a forged document, whatever it might be, this was the place to come. They didn't sell directly to the public. They dealt with herders at the park, independents who screened the customers to make sure they were not *placas*, or undercover cops.

Reymundo saw the flow of commerce first hand; he watched intently and did not miss any moves. He was piecing everything and everyone together. He thought for a moment, tilted his head slightly, grimaced, and said to himself, "Hmm, now that I can do." He stuffed the paper in the garbage can along with the water bottle, brushed off his hands on his lap, got up and walked towards a storefront. He went back to the trash can to grab the paper to cover his head; it had started to rain.

One month later Reymundo was wearing a fake Rolex and cheap gold rings. He wore a loud colored silk shirt from the swap meet, which he wore open with a white wife beater underneath. His hair was slicked back; he had lamb chop side burns and a cool goatee. He wore shiny silver polyester pants and rattlesnake boots. He brought in more business than three stores could handle. He had a one-bedroom studio apartment, which he called a bachelor's pad, two blocks away, and when he was not at the park you could find him at a watering hole simply called La Bar.

It was called La Bar because of the use of Spanglish throughout South Cali, but also because it sounded like the word for 'to wash or *lavar*' in Spanish, so when somebody asked, "Hey, where's Fulano De Tal?" one could simply say, "*Se fue a* La Bar," which sounded like they were saying, "He went to wash." That made Fulano sound like such a responsible individual. "Wow, that Fulano is such a hard-working guy, he washes clothes night after night!"

Reymundo spent most of his money on liquor and whores; the good life. He dabbled in anything he could snort; partied like he was going to go to prison the next day. On one Saturday night, Reymundo was at La Bar enjoying his favorite beer and cocktail – Miller Genuine Draft in a bottle and shots of tequila *La Cabrita* – and chain smoking Marlboro Lights. He was sitting at his own personal bar stool, accompanied by a woman who looked as though she'd been really good looking at one time, but now booze had sucked the life out of her. She was his neighbor. The jukebox was playing *"Nieves de Enero"* by Chalino Sanchez, Reymundo's favorite drinking song.

The woman was telling Reymundo that she was thinking about moving farther north to work with her sister in a bar called Chato's Cantina, outside of Eugene, Oregon. She could no longer stand living in LA since she'd busted her live-in boyfriend in bed with an underage girl.

She was asking for him for a hundred dollar loan for a bus ticket, and promised to repay him as soon as she got her first check. Reymundo did not hesitate to take his big leather wallet out and give her two crisp hundred-dollar bills. He handed the money to her, but told her that he was giving it to her under the condition that she have one last shot with him.

She laughingly agreed, wiping tears from her eyes as they both took a shot. She bit into a lemon, and he drank his straight up, no citrus fruit, as always. A commotion was heard outside. Somebody yelled, *"La migra!"* and the bar emptied out. Reymundo and the woman also ran out, but in opposite directions. She went the wrong way.

Reymundo was able to get away, he was in the clear but felt guilty for leaving her behind. Reymundo went back for his friend, whom he found fighting with an LAPD officer. They both got arrested for disturbing the peace and thrown into Los Angeles County Jail. As quickly as Reymundo had risen to the top, his life in the fast lane had ended.

Templo del Mundo

Reymundo sat in a jail cell contemplating his trials and tribulations; he realized all the pain of the community all around him, his *raza,* people who would have been his sheep had he still been in the business of leading lost souls to salvation. There was no one there to guide the youth. Single mothers living on welfare, children being raised with the spirituality of tennis shoes and video games. He felt guilty for his turn to debauchery, and wished he could help. He prayed to God like he had when he was young, before he was a priest.

He had a deep, soulful conversation with the creator. He apologized for his fall from grace and asked for forgiveness. He promised that if God delivered him once more, he would never fall again. Then, realizing that not falling from grace was not for him to promise, he changed his request, saying he would "try" to remain fixated on helping his own people in their struggle; the lost people of the sun.

He was released from jail the next day. He was surprised that his documents were not questioned. He walked down the jailhouse steps and onto the sidewalk, looked up toward the sky, made the sign of the cross and headed out, to anywhere. As he walked, marveling at his blessings, he was full of hope. He now knew that God had shined a light on him. He felt the warmth of faith covering him like a protective blanket. He noticed young a woman with a baby; she was distraught.

He approached her and asked her about her grief. She told him in Spanish that her husband had spent her entire savings on booze and drugs; Reymundo himself began to feel a bit guilty as he listened. The husband had run off with another woman, and she had been evicted from her weekly hotel with her 1-year-old daughter.

He tried to calm her down, promising to get her help, explaining to her that governmental agencies could help her. She vehemently rejected going to any authorities because she had no *papeles*. He assured her that she would be fine. He told her that he had promised God that he would do a good deed for helping him out of... a predicament. He gave her the money he had in his pocket for food for the baby. He took her on the bus to the welfare office.

He filled out the required paperwork, and after a two-hour wait they were called into an office. He translated for her, and explained that she was his cousin. She was a single mother, destitute, and had been robbed of her identification. He used his mastery of the tongue and gained favor with the welfare social worker, who had now taken pity on the poor woman.

The social worker decided to help Reymundo's "cousin" Ermelinda, "Tell her she has to get an address within the next twenty-four hours. I can give her a check today and food stamps will come in the mail. Thank you, Mr. Ochoa. She can pick up her check at the window outside my office in fifteen minutes, they'll call out her name." Reymundo was surprised, but didn't show it. He escorted Ermelinda out of the office.

"Que te dijieron Reymundo? Me van a deportar? Por favor dime algo." "Ermelinda," said Reymundo, *"no te van a deportar, te van ayudar."* A tear streamed down her cheek. She looked at him as if he were a savior. She was thankful that her gamble on this stranger hadn't gone wrong. She was sure this was sign from God, that he was a man sent by God to help her.

"Ermelinda Martinez," cried a voice from a speaker. "Ermelinda Lindazo Martinez to the window, please!"
Reymundo and Ermelinda walked up to the window. "Are you her husband?" asked the clerk.

"No, no, I am her cousin, her translator," replied Reymundo. "Okay, tell her to sign here, here, and here, and initial in these two places here." The clerk ripped off the bottom portion and handed a check to a very surprised Ermelinda. Ermelinda's eyes widened when she saw the check. She didn't know how to read, but surely knew numbers. Eight hundred forty-seven dollars and seventy-two cents. She held her hands to her mouth and began to cry.

She knew that her life had just taken a turn for the better. The clerk was surprised by this and realized that she had just saved this woman's life. "Thenk ju, thenk ju," said Ermelinda.

The clerk smiled, knowing that this would be the highlight of her day. She was accustomed to rude women with a sense of entitlement demanding their monthly checks. But these were the moments she lived for. "You are welcome, Mrs. Martinez. Now go take care of your baby. Bye bye, now."

Reymundo and Ermelinda stepped out of the welfare office; she was holding the baby in a bundle along with her life's belongings. Reymundo helped her with some bags. He explained that she needed to be careful with this money, and that he would take her to get it cashed at a liquor store so she could put a deposit on a small studio apartment.

Ermelinda's eyes were awash with tears; she looked at her savior, and could not believe that God had sent him to her. "*Gracias, Don Reymundo, gracias a Dios, no se como te lo podre agradecer, gracias.*"

The Templo del Mundo was a loosely organized Christian church serving the El Sereno community of East Los Angeles. Everyone in the world was welcome, hence the name, *Templo del Mundo*. Padre Mundo was holding his Tuesday night Mass.

Padre Mundo gave an unscripted sermon with stories and testaments revolving around songs praising the Lord to more than two hundred people packed into an old abandoned movie theatre. Padre Mundo was well known among the community. Everyone loved him; he spoke the truth, told it like it was.

Reymundo was not afraid to tell the community leaders where they fell short on helping the people. The big, fancy Christian churches found Reymundo to be a thorn in their side, as he lured away the followers who used to fill their donation baskets. They conspired among each other, and one evening a report came into the immigration office that Padre Mundo was promising citizenship to illegals, going as far as giving them false papers to stay in the country while they supposedly waited for amnesty. The report was not entirely false.

The following week, seven California Border Patrol vans raided Templo del Mundo's Sunday Holy Mass. The people scrimmaged around, kids were crying, men ran about every which way, people falling down, while the echoing sounds of batons hitting skulls created a terrible scene. Reymundo was horrified as he stood and watched everything crumble right in front of his eyes.

Two burly officers approached him. They asked for his documentation. When Reymundo gave them his forged documents he was handcuffed with large zip ties and loaded into an awaiting van. He was taken to an immigration holding tank in Blythe, California, near the Arizona-California border.

At the detention facility, Reymundo began to question himself and his life. He was not yet ready to give up, but had serious faith issues. He slowly and quietly prayed to the God who had so gently led him through so much pain. "Seven times you will fall," he heard a voice say from the other side of the bars. It was Sister Leslie Anderson of the Sisters of the Calvary Baptist Church of the Greater Blythe Area. "But if you get up that eighth time you still have hope!" she preached.

"Hallelujah! Preach on sister!" her church sisters encouraged her. She looked Reymundo directly in the eyes as she talked. "You came here for answers and wound up in this hell hole. Go home, son, and live a good, honest life in your own country. I come with the message of peace from the Lord Almighty especially for you, Señor!

Go back to your country, your home, and be with God. I come with a message… and some food and clothing!" She broke into a funny laugh then began to hand out sandwiches, shirts, socks and hats to the migrants being processed for deportation.

She handed Reymundo an old, blue baseball cap and told him, "Here you go, son, it will keep the hot sun from your head and your hair from going all over the place, it'll give you a sense of dignity at a time when you most need it. Here, it's for you, from God, I come with a message," she said and moved along to the next person.

Reymundo grabbed the sandwich and the hat. He looked at the old blue hat, then noticed the logo on the front and stopped dead in his tracks. It was a San Diego Padres hat, and right in the front was none other than The Swinging Friar. The club-wielding Padre bashing away the sins of the world.

Surely it was a sign, a message, as sister Anderson had proclaimed, and that message was surely for him. He was reinvigorated. He knew that God had not abandoned him but merely changed his course. Everything was going to be okay; he ate the sandwich and fell into a sweet sleep, wearing his hat, which fit his big head perfectly.

Inkopah

The van stopped for its final break off an exit near a mountain town outside San Diego called Inkopah. Sergeant Rob went inside to pay for the gas. When the doors of the van opened, the prisoners stumbled out hungry and thirsty. Officer Jack was up to his antics; he was trying to get a rise out of Psyko, but the young man's compatriots urged Psyko to hold his tongue.

"Cholo calmate no vale la pena ese guey," said Luis.
As Psyko walked towards the restroom with the others in single file, Officer Jack slid his baton between the backs of Psyko's legs, brushing his buttocks as he said in a low, menacing voice, "You're my bitch now!"

Psyko lost control. "Come on, *puto,* you want a piece of me?" He raised powerful fists behind his head as if to strike, and Officer Jack flinched like a girl and covered himself with both hands outstretched, turning his face away. The detainees erupted in laughter but quickly stopped as they realized the wrath that would surely follow. Officer Jack's eyes widened in anger as he realized he'd just been punked.

Officer Jack drew back his club as far as he could and delivered the hardest blow he could muster, but not before Luis jumped in front of Psyko, shielding him but receiving the blow directly upon the temple. Luis fell to the ground, unconscious. Sergeant Rob saw the commotion and yelled to Jack, who acted like it was no big deal, shrugging and mumbling. "He got in the way, boss… They were gonna… Aw, you know it's not my fault, man!" The other aliens huddled together in disbelief, traumatized by what they had just witnessed.

Sergeant Rob tried to bring the young man to consciousness. He cleaned off the blood and softly slapped his cheek, calling, "Luis! Luis! Can you hear me, son?" Sergeant Rob tried his hardest to bring back Luis; he shook him and pleaded with him. "Come on, boy, wake up! You'll be okay. *Andale muchacho!*"

With the smell of jasmine in the lazy afternoon, Luis was transported to his home in South Carolina. He was flying through the air to the sound of Amador Adanowsky's "*Saber Amar*," his arms outstretched like a bird. Through the clouds, he looked down upon the South Carolina ranch he left behind. He saw the horses running and turned like a plane making coordinate changes.

He glided down and was riding a beautiful white Pegasus with large lovely wings. They were gliding alongside the running horses in green pastures. Luis motioned to the horses as if to dare them to race him; the horses obliged, the race was on, and then he was leading them, a million horses behind him. Luis took a deep breath, extended his arm outward, looked up into the sky and took in the moment as the flying horse continued a fervent pace.

Luis flew back up and around like an eagle high above. He saw the main house and Don Bob waving; he turned the Pegasus and went down to say hello. He approached Don Bob. "Come on, Luey!" yelled Don Bob to a surprised Luis. *How can this be? Don Bob is dead, I saw it with my own eyes*, Luis thought, but he was relieved to be back home, safe and sound, in good old South Carolina.

"Yeah, boy, weezah gonna have a good old fashioned home town hoe down for your coming home, bar-be-cue, fiddlahs and banjos, just like we use to do. Remembah?" said Don Bob to Luis as he handed him a bottle of his finest Kentucky Bourbon.

Luis took a chug and was overpowered by the strong alcohol as he always did. They all laughed at the boy's fumblings with the bottle. "Yah raised a fine horseman, Don Miguel!" Don Bob said.

Luis looked over and saw his Tata Miguel as tears rolled down his face. "Tata! You are here!" He walked toward his grandfather, who had passed away twelve years ago, with open arms. Grandpa Miguel, with a big smile, proudly hugged his grandson who was so good with horses. He held him by the shoulder and looked at him and said, "*Muchacho! Muchacho! Muchacho!*"

Luis came into consciousness. He opened his eyes and let out a low grufflegarl. He was being shaken by Sergeant Rob. "Thank God. I thought we lost you, boy," Rob said. Luis rolled into and out of consciousness but assured the Sarge that he was okay. "Come on. You can sit up front here with me. Nobody is going to lay a finger on you," Rob said as he looked at Jack.

Jack turned away as he mumbled under his breath, "It was an accident." Sergeant Rob helped Luis into the front seat and strapped the middle seat belt on him. After everyone was boarded, they went on their way.

The officers forgot to gas up the van rolled off; the mood was somber. Reymundo switched his seat and slid next to Nelly. He put his arm around her to console her. She had become very attached to Luis. "Did you see what they did to poor Ranas?" she said.

"Yes, *mija,* I saw. A little part of me died when I heard the crack of his skull."
"Hey, Reymundo, why don't you continue that story about the Aztec people?" Pretty Boy prodded.
"I don't know. Maybe Luis would have wanted to hear it," responded Reymundo.
"Come on, tell us," Nelly said, hitting Reymundo playfully in the side with her elbow.
"Okay, you win," said Reymundo.

The Rise and Fall of Aztatlan VI – The Conquest of Anahuac

After many months of travel, the entire Mexica nation arrived in the valley of Anahuac. They arrived at the outskirts of the Azcapotzalco. They were met by the chief elders, who had heard about the Mexica exploits and their fierce, unstoppable war machine. The Azcapotzalco controlled much of the valley, though they were in a constant state of war. The nations made peace and a pact of wartime allegiance. The Mexica continued on until they come upon a piece of land in the marshes, by Lake Texcoco.

Mexitli stopped his people, and the entire Mexica nation waited to learn what had held their migration. Mexitli summoned the elders and chiefs of war. It was an eagle, perched atop a rock where the cactus grew; the eagle held a rattlesnake in its clutches. The Mexica had finally arrived at their promised land. The Azcapotzalco allowed the Mexica to settle on this lake. The lake did not have any value to the Azcapotzalco; the area was uninhabitable.

The Mexica, a hard-working, resourceful people, designed a way to fill the shallow lake with mud and build it up until they could create a passageway on the lake. They created a maze of roads with mud and stones and dirt. It was truly an engineering feat. In the center they marked off an entire area that would serve as their metropolis. They were going to create a city atop a lake. They worked nonstop. The men dug and carried, the women as well, and they worked together as a nation should.

When the land on top of the lake was firm and inhabitable, they set their sights on the surrounding resources of stone and rock which they quarried to build a temple to the two Gods who had seen them through battle and showed the way; Huitzilopochtli and Tlaloc. They built an amazing giant pyramid made of stone, which was taller than any structure in the entire surrounding land. They built a giant city, and the people of the Sun God prospered.

People came from many miles around to pay tribute; tribes wanted to form alliances with the new warrior nation. The Mexica conquered surrounding areas and created alliances within the tribes, including Xocimilco and Tlacopan. Azcapotzalco, however, refused to pay tribute or be conquered. They were used to being the ruling tribe of the area, although they were in constant war with their neighbors.

When the leader of the Azcapotzalco died, his son, Maxtla, assumed the throne. He put forth a plan that his father before him had rejected. He would finish off the Mexica by cutting off the head of the snake; Maxtla sent a hit squad to assassinate Tenoch.

Disguised as tributes, the Tepanec emissaries of the Azcapotzalco Nation were given full escorts into Tenochtitlan. When they arrived at the high temple, the ruler, Tenoch, having prepared for sacrifice, was in a hallucinogenic state. The assassins struck with lances and knives but were immediately cut down by the multitudes of guards protecting Tenoch. Tenoch went down, but he did not die.

Tenoch immediately waged war on the Azcapotzalco, whose leader went into exile to the south, toward modern-day Guatemala. The ferocity of the Mexica had reached a new level. The two main tribes, the largest in the area, announced a truce and requested absolute allegiance with the Mexica. Tenoch met with the two leaders of Texcoco and Tlacopan. They formed what was to be known in history as the Aztec Triple Alliance of Tenochtitlan, Texcoco, and Tlacopan.

The Triple Alliance was the most powerful nation of North America. All other tribes were tributary states. However, Tenochtitlan had greater influence and eventually led the three nations for hundreds of years. They sacrificed thousands of brave warriors to the Sun God, who in turn helped the Aztec Empire maintain its power for a long time. The leadership of the Aztecs varied from generation to generation.

The rulers, or *tlahtoani*, of the mighty Aztec Empire were as follows: Mexitli led the Mexica through the years of wandering; Tenoch in the year 1325; Acamapichtli from 1375 to 1395; Huitzilihuitli from 1396 to 1417; Chimalpopca from 1417 to 1426; Itzcoatl from 1427 to 1440; Moctezuma from 1440 to 1469; Axayacatl from 1469 to 1481; Tizoc from 1481 to 1486; Ahuitzotl from 1486 to 1502; Moctezuma II from 1502 to 1520; Cuitlahuac 1520; and Cuauhtémoc from 1520 to 1521.

Toward the end of the Aztec Empire, the visions and the sacrifices to the Sun God Huitzilopochtli gave way to a new God; the Son of Man. The people of the sun would soon find their real God, the Son of Man, who would form a very special bond with the children of the Aztec people. In 1521, the Spanish arrived in the New World. The Aztec people, expecting the arrival of the new God, welcomed the Conquistadors with open arms.

That did not end well for the leaders of the Aztec Empire. The history books would document a one-sided encounter favoring the Spaniards. One interesting tidbit is the legend of El Dorado. The Spaniards, being gold thirsty, and seeing that the Aztecs had a source of gold, figured that there must have been a treasure trove of gold somewhere in the kingdom. When stories of the fabled land of Aztlan, or Aztatlan, with its paradise-like existence, were overheard by the Spaniards, they were sure that this would be the place where they would find the mother lode.

The Spaniards pinpointed, as best they could, the legendary place of origin of the Aztecs, Aztlan, to be to the northwest near a body of water. They sent expeditions towards the Pacific Ocean, towards California, by way of Baja California and Arizona. This they did in the name of the church, but really, the quests were to find the golden city of El Dorado.

That is why today you find so many Spanish names on West Coast of the United States, specifically in California. Names like San Francisco, San Diego, Los Angeles, Chula Vista, Sacramento, San

Jose, Santa Ana, Modesto, San Bernardino, Santa Cruz, Moreno
Valley, Santa Clarita, Rancho Cucamonga, Corona, Salinas,
Pasadena, Escondido, El Cajon, El Centro, Temecula, Santa Maria,
San Mateo, Vista, Mission Viejo, Vacaville, Santa Monica, Santa
Barbara, Chico, San Marcos, Chino, and El Segundo, to name a few.

Reymundo finished the story when he noticed that the van was
pulling off the highway.

"I feel like I have to pray or something. I'm confused. I am in a bad
place in my head, Reymundo," admitted Nelly.
"So pray, or just talk to Him," said Reymundo.
"Talk to whom? I'm not Catholic. I don't even know how to make
the sign of the cross," said Nelly.

"Listen, *cielito lindo*, I am neither Catholic, nor Christian, nor
Jewish, nor Islamist, Buddhist, nor even a Scientologist. I am a child
of God, bright like one of His millions of shining stars that adorn His
beautiful sky twinkling bright for the whole world to see," said the
old, former man of the cloth.
"What are we doing? We're almost there," cried Jack, upset.
"Well, unless you want to walk, we are running out of gas," said
Sergeant Rob.

"Didn't you just put gas in at the last stop?" asked Jack.
"If remember correctly, Jack, I never got a chance to gas up since
you were back there playing piñata with this poor boy. You okay?"
Sergeant Rob asked Luis. The young man looked up, eyes half-open,
and gurgled an almost incoherent "Okay," and fell back into
unconsciousness.

The van pulled into a service station, Valero Gas, off Tavern Road
in Alpine; they were forty-five minutes from downtown San Diego
and one hour from the border. Sergeant Rob got out to pay and pump
gas, except this time nobody else was allowed to get out, only Jack,

who was ordered to stay by his sergeant's side. Rob told Jack to pump the gas.

Reymundo continued his talk: "… We are directly connected to the creator; I can sense him all around me. And because we are connected to Him we have his undivided attention at any moment, anywhere in time. We can speak with Him about anything. Come on, we'll talk to Him together…." He was interrupted by the loud thumping sound approaching.

A white Cadillac Escalade with white and chrome twenty-six inch rims pulled up to the island next to the van, blasting loud music through a high performance sound system. A young, good looking black man, about 18 years old, wearing a white hoodie, white baggy jeans, and white tennis shoes, with a white bandana hanging out of his left back pocket, was bejeweled with platinum rings, chains, and diamond earrings. He stepped out and walked inside with rhythmic steps that seemed to go with the music. He left the keys in the car and the loud music could clearly be heard like a concert performance.

Everyone in the van looked intensely at the young man, in awe of his persona, his ride, his beautiful young ebony girlfriend who was more concerned with primping her hair in the mirror and ensuring her nails were as radiant as ever. They imagined themselves in his position; jaws dropped.

The song ended and a new song began. It was Al Green's "How Can You Mend A Broken Heart." As the song played, Padre Mundo continued his conversation with Nelly. Al Green provided an interesting and appropriate background that seemed to somehow verify all that Reymundo was conveying to Nelly, and for all those in the van who understood English – even Sergeant Rob – the moment was captivating as the informal sermon intertwined in a ballet of words and music:

"I think about when I was a kid and all I wanted was to be like my father, get a job like my father, it's what was expected of you. I could never decide what to do with my life, much less where I was headed. And certainly no one told me about the pain and struggles which I was about to face or guided me in a direction in which to go...."

The first lyrics of the Al Green song coincided with the words spoken by Reymundo.

"...Oh Lord, how can we overcome these trials, our burdens have overrun us, how can you stop these tears from flowing, who can stop the Son of Man from lighting our souls, oh please Lord, I beg of you, your son Mundo, how can I continue on?...."

The lyrics of the song continued to mimic the words the old man said as he prayed with Nelly and all those who had come this far. "How can this young man..." Reymundo motioned with his hand towards Psyko, who was caught off guard, "... serve your purpose? What is your plan for him? Can this sinner ever be forgiven? Is he worthy, Lord? Oh, Lord, save him, save me, I want to be in your grace again...."

The words and the lyrics of the song were so uplifting and inspiring that those understood them in English were in awe of what they were witnessing.

"...The spirit of the almighty is all around us..." Reymundo waved his hand toward some trees in the distance, "...but we can only think about our own selfish needs and self-pity, a self-pity that blinds us and robs us of your presence. Why, Lord, does no one take the time to help each other, lend an ear, give good advice, Lord...."

The song continued its lyrical ballet, surely a divine message to those who had suffered so much.

"...I beg of you to calm my soul, and I am a sinner, Lord, not worthy of you to come into my heart, but one word from you, Lord, is enough to save me. Who can keep us from ever crying again?...."

Everyone in the van was in a hypnotic trance from Reymundo's words and how they blended with the sounds of the soulful music, and they began to wave their arms in the air in a synchronized rhythm reminiscent of a Baptist church revival.

"...Who can prevent the Son of Man from illuminating the universe, what is the reason for our being....'

Yes, it was a divine message. Al Green was the prophet who sang the words that mimicked the ex-preacher's prayers, prayers that came from a people with a rich history who were now reduced to illegals and treated as less than dogs.

"...After all is said and done, I can only sing your hymns, oh Lord...."

The young, beautiful black girl in the Escalade sang along with the song while updating her social web page. She noticed the van occupants waving their hands in the air and chuckled to herself, amused. She put her hand out the window and joined in, while continuing to sing along with the Reverend Al Green. Her boyfriend, looking through the window of the minimart while paying for his gas, saw her and waved back, assuming she was so smitten by him that she missed him so.

The words of the beautiful song being played in the young black man's car were a testament to the prayers from Reymundo's soul. The song danced in the air and in their souls, cementing their hearts together in a moment that would never be forgotten.

Psyko, caught up in the moment, began to pray to God. "Dear Father, who is, I mean art, in heaven… I have done so much evil, I know that I admit it, God, can I ever be forgiven?" Psyko continued his prayer. "Lord, please, I want to be saved, I have this strong feeling. Ranas never did nothing wrong, I would like to help him, I want to be saved."

His prayers came with background music that would continue to set the stage for a real conversion of the soul. Psyko knew that this was meant to be. Never in his wildest dreams had he ever thought he would experience this. What it was he did not know, but he knew that if there were a God, this would be his way of speaking to Him.

"Lord, I'm surely not worthy of your attention. How can I be fixed? There is no hope for me, I, I feel I want to save my soul but I feel I am beyond redemption." He began to cry. "*Pero yo se que*, I know, no, I promise that if you save me, rescue me today, I will live a full life dedicated to your word, yes Lord, I want your salvation, I repent from all the evil I have caused the world. Although I am but a lowly wetback, a *mojado*, please Lord, accept me, Lord. Send me a sign, Lord."

He cried hard, not worried about who would see him.
The clouds above broke open, revealing a glimpse of the sun and providing a comfortable breeze through the windows of the van.
As the song finished there was excitement in the air, a newfound spirituality that could never be taken away. What the people at that moment experienced could never be explained, not in regular talk or layman's terms. "You had to be there," they would all say later when asked to retell the golden moment.

The young man returned from the minimart with a bottle of strawberry soda and a bag of Lay's Bar-B-Que potato chips for his girlfriend and a can of Arizona Iced Tea and a bag of Skittles for himself. His girlfriend told him, "Trey, shoulda seen those *eses* in that van there getting all soulful and shit right now, just like in church, hands in the air and everything. It was pretty cool though, I thought."

Trey adjusted his rear view mirror to check his fade and mumbled to her under his breath. "Oh yeah? That's cool, let's get the hell out of here. This ain't no place for a young black man to be." He started his car as the music, which was already winding down, stopped and was followed by loud gangsta rap. Trey looked back, then side to side, put a joint in his mouth, lit it with an ivory and chrome lighter, took a couple puffs, and turned his head towards the van next to him. He looked up to Psyko, whose eyes were locked on him, and nodded as if to say, "This one's for you, *ese.*" He winked and sped away towards the Pacific Ocean with the beautiful San Diego skyline at its feet.

In the van, which was now headed west on Highway 8, Nelly looked at Reymundo. "That was beautiful, you must be a really good preacher." She felt a new sense of calm and dozed off leaning on one of the big man's enormous shoulders. The van continued on its way, but this time there was no singing or laughter or fighting or cursing. Heading south on Interstate 5, Psyko motioned to Reymundo. "*Mira,* Padre, Friar, *alla esta tu canton,* there over west, that's Petco Park, that's where the Padres play." Psyko was telling Reymundo that the stadium where the Padres played was Reymundo's house, a play on words regarding the friar and the preacher.

Reymundo seemed confused. "They play *futbol?*" asked the big man. "No, man, you're wearing a San Diego Padres hat, and that's the stadium the Padres play at. I thought it was pretty cool, that's all," answered Psyko.

"Yes, that's very cool, Eriberto, the lights of the arena are beautiful, and they look like diamonds in the night sky. Is there a game right now?" Reymundo didn't get the connection, but he didn't want to discourage Psyko's enthusiasm. He'd never seen a baseball game in his life. He smiled at Psyko and went back to his conversation with Nelly.

It was 5 p.m. and Marty was driving like a maniac down Interstate 5, already near downtown San Diego. He had made it in four hours and had avoided being pulled over, a feat in itself. They spotted the van heading south in National City, a small city within San Diego County, ten minutes south of downtown SD. Marty pulled alongside the van on the driver's side. Darlene held the legal paperwork to the window and motioned for the driver to pull over so they could explain and intercept the deportation.

Sergeant Rob was not about to disregard the orders he had been given. By now he had figured out why this special trip was taking place, and he was not about to blow this very important assignment. Sargeant Rob motioned to Darlene with an absolute "No." The sarge was obviously very angry at the intruding car. He would not pull over or be outsmarted by a couple of young girls and their friend. He continued on and radioed ahead in case the crazy girls and their driver in the Mustang tried anything funny. In Chula Vista, a police car pulled alongside the van and escorted it the rest of the way.

Marty continued on. He figured there was no way this official was going to let Nelly go, even with a legal document. His best bet was to cross into Mexico and wait for her, or risk being arrested at the border.

As the van drove down the highway, Psyko saw a billboard. "Aztec Football: Get your tickets now." He read the billboard and asked Reymundo, "How does that story end, the one about our people?" Reymundo eloquently replies "That my young Aztec Prince is up to you, you see the Aztec lives inside you and although we no longer use that blood thirst for evil we must turn it into something else, we must use the clever tools and be part of this system. The Sun God Huitzilopochtli left long ago. He had his time but his time was then, he made way for the new God of the son. The Son of Man Jesus Christ our only savior. Ours is the story of sadness, of a warrior nation misunderstood.

The true lost tribe resides inside of you. You Eriberto, must dig inside your soul and decide if you get beat, or will you summon the Azteca within and be part of this great society and be a role model for those young Latinos who will eventually fall prey to the gangs and drugs. The Son of Man needs his warriors for a war that won't be fought with spears, arrows, knives, or even guns, this war being waged on the young people of America, Mexico, all over the world is a true war of good versus evil. What side you choose to be on is up to you. Will you take the lessons learned, ask forgiveness and join the plight of the oppressed or will you join the evil one in his pursuit of destruction of the people of the Son of Man."

Psyko was listening to Reymundo talk about his faith, his Aztec research, and his advice to the young Hispanic. "Reymundo, you are my true road dog, How do you say dog in the Aztec language?" asked Psyko.

"*Itzcuintli,* that's dog in Nahuatl, the language spoken by the Azteca. Now, if you want to refer to the traditional Mexican hairless, or the Aztec dog, you would say *xoloitzcuintle!*" replied Reymundo. "Xolo?" asked Psyko. "Like a gangster *cholo?*"

"Yes, it's pronounced the same, but it's spelled with the letter X," Reymundo corrected the curious young man.

"So if I see a homie and I want to say 'What's up, dog?' I could simply say 'What's up xolo... squeekly?'" Psyko twisted up the word. "Yeah, something like that," replied Reymundo as Psyko practiced his new Aztec word.

Welcome to Tijuana

The van pulled up to the Port of Entry, ready to unload the undocumented migrants. When the van stopped, a Border Patrol agent greeted them and directed them towards the unloading area. Even before the van got close to the gate, you could hear the steady, rhythmic "Clack Clack Clack Clack Clack" of the metal revolving door that sounded every time someone passed through it. It was a steady flow, and rarely did the sound ever stop. This was the door into Mexico. One could only imagine the sound the figurative revolving door coming into America would make; it would probably sound something like an Uzi machine gun that never ran out of ammunition.

Sergeant Rob was worried. He spoke quietly to the officer in charge, who automatically shook his head and ground his teeth. "No way, man, uh-uh. You better walk right over to the Federales and explain your situation." Sergeant Rob did as he was advised. He walked towards the Mexican side and summoned a dark Mexican man from the *Aduana* (Customs) and asked him to fetch his commanding officer. The young man did.

The Mexican officer in charge seemed upset, but in the end he agreed to whatever it was that was requested of him. Sergeant Rob motioned to Jack, who immediately headed to the cab of the van to pull out Luis. He motioned to an ambulance EMT who had just arrived. The illegal aliens still locked in the back looked intensely at what was going on. Nobody said a word.

They placed the young man on a gurney and rolled him towards the Mexican side. The Mexican *jefe* looked at the young man, shook his head in pity and covered the boy's face by placing a sheet over his head. Nelly gasped in horror. She couldn't breathe. She covered her face and immediately turned around in the opposite direction, closed her eyes, put her head down, and began to cry. The Mexican *jefe* motioned to his underlings to roll the body away.

"They killed him. They killed Ranas, the bastards," Nelly cried in a squeaky, sorrowful voice with her eyes closed. "And not one person will do anything about it!" She continued to weep until she heard the sound of the doors swinging open and saw the light shining through. *"Ya llegamos amigos."* Sergeant Rob, oblivious to his riders' grief, tried to lighten the mood. He had sent Jack Gutierrez to file the paperwork mainly so that the aliens could have a final moment of dignity. They had seen the last of Jack Gutierrez.

Nelly was the first to stagger out, slowly, tears rolling down her face. She looked straight ahead like a convict walking toward her execution. She walked hesitantly to the swinging, clacking, revolving gate, then with renewed courage she marched right up to the door. She suddenly stopped. She turned around and took one last look at the country that had raised her, the country that was now rejecting her and sending to the wolves. She took a deep breath, the last she would take on American soil. She pushed the door, which responded with a resounding "clack," and she walked into Mexico for the first time in ten years.

There was a table with Mexican officials who greeted and questioned each deported person away from the regular flow of incoming tourists and citizens. It was a sort of screening for illegal monies or wanted felons and, of course, deported paisanos.

Nelly walked straight up to the first official. *"Que es tu nombre, señorita?"* An overweight bureaucrat never looked up from his clipboard as he asked for her name. He wore a tight, white government-issue button-down polyester shirt. "Nayeli Itzel de Coyotaxtli Jimenez," Nelly responded. The man slowly raised his head. Was she for real? The padre, who was right behind her, was gleaming with joy as if to exclaim, "She has come home; she was once lost, but now she's found!"

"Hmm," the official said as he jotted something down. He stamped a piece of paper, then tore off the top sheet, handed it to her and said,

"Beinvenidos a Mexico, Paisana." Welcome, compatriot. He tossed his head as if to show her the direction into Mexico.

She noticed some waving hands and saw Marty and her friends waiting in Mexico. They ran towards each other, crying. They melted into one big group hug. Marty held the little black box in his pocket, waiting for the right moment to offer his own solution; he took it out of his pocket secretly. There was so much to say and explain. They told her they had petitioned the courts and that she would be back in no time.

"I am not going back," she said, to the amazement of her pals. "What do you mean?" they all asked. "When I return to the United States, I will return on my terms... and as citizen of Mexico." Her friends were shocked, but they were happy for her; they realized that she wasn't as traumatized as they had expected, and that she had changed for the better. She was no longer afraid.

Marty slid the ring back into his coat pocket; afraid that someone might see it. Nelly turned back towards Psyko, worried for him; would they arrest him and beat him?

"Do you know that guy?" asked Darlene. "My God, he looks scary, you poor thing. In that van with all those crazy lowlifes, OMG." They clutched their collective chests and offered more support.

Nelly responded to them, but mostly to herself, as she kept her gaze on Psyko. "He's not crazy; he's just a guy, just another person like you and me. Come on, let's get out of here. I have to find a place, I need to take a hot shower." They walked off as a hugging group, talking, chatting, excited. The end to their problems was close at hand, thank God.

The padre looked towards them with satisfaction, like a shepherd who had watched over his flock but had now turned it over to the next shift. *"Su nombre?"* The official again asked Reymundo for his name.

The padre addressed the official. "*Oh, perdon, Padre Raymmm....*"
He stopped in midsentence. "*Disculpe, Reymundo Ochoa Lopez
Lopez.*"

At the next table, a thin middle-aged woman who appeared to take
her job seriously asked Doña Rosa the same question. "*Su nombre
por favor?*"

Doña Rosa responded, "*Socorro Baltzar Baca del Corral.*"
Psyko was taken by three armed soldiers from the *Marina Mexicana*.
He was flanked with a soldier on each side. They roughed him up a
bit to intimidate him, to no avail. He heard Reymundo's voice in his
head: "*Esos gueyes no valen la pena Cholo!*" – they are not worth it.
He took his abuse like a man. "*De donde vienes?*" (Where are you
coming from?) "*Tienes drogas?*" (Do you have drugs?) "*Tienes
antespenales?*" (Do you have a record?) They riddled him with
question after question. They led him towards the gurney which held
the body of Ranas and asked Psyko, "Do you know this man?"
"No," Psyko calmly stated.

They barked in Spanish, "Did you have anything to do with this?"
"No," repeated Psyko. "You don't know this man?" they asked a
third time. "No!" said Psyko for the last time.

"*Andale pues*," they said – okay then – and they let him go.
While the soldiers were distracted, Psyko took the leather strap
necklace with the wooden "L" from around Ranas's neck. He put it
in his pocket as he was shoved on his way into Tijuana. As he
walked off, he stopped, took the necklace out of his pocket, and
looked at the only memento he had of the man who had saved his
life. It wasn't a wooden "L" at all, but the remaining fragments of a
broken cross. Psyko tied it around his own neck, gently touched it
with his hand against his chest, and closed his eyes.

He knew he had barely escaped doom in a Mexican prison, and he
bravely walked towards a country he didn't remember, a world he'd

never known. As he walked down the sidewalk leading into downtown Tijuana, he saw Nelly in the back seat of Marty's car, with Darlene riding shotgun. He looked at Nelly, she looked at him; there were no words or goodbyes, and they both realized they had never known each other after all.

As she went by she saw he was wearing Luis's wooden "L" around his neck. Her eyes lit up as if she wanted to say something, but the car had already gone too far.

Psyko heard somebody call his name; it was Pretty Boy and Yeyo. Pretty Boy told Psyko that he and Yeyo were going to make the trek back into California the next day. He had a friend nearby and towards the east in a place called El Nido where many tunnels existed; Yeyo was heading up to Gualala, California, to work for him. He offered Psyko the same deal.

Psyko told Pretty Boy that he was going to stay in Tijuana for now, and joked about running into his father. Pretty Boy wrote down his address and told Psyko that if he ever went up to Northern Cali to be sure and look him up so they could have a smoke out. Psyko laughed and said "*Orale!* (All right.) You got it homie." They all shook hands and parted ways.

As Psyko walked away he could be heard singing a rap tune he had just created:

> *I'm crossing dope through the sierra, getting clothes*
> *full a tierra, twenty more miles 'fore I get to the*
> *frontera.*
>
> *Mules a packing like a bitch, they never gettin rich,*
> *I'm up in my pad not a worry not a hitch.*
>
> *We're the People of the Sun, our time has just*
> *begun, pass the thirteenth Baktun, so include the*
> *previous one.*

We're the people, the people, the people of the sun.
Tatted up, tatted up, tatted up, tatted up

We're the people, the people, the people of the sun.
Tatted up, tatted up, tatted up, tatted up

We're the people, the people, the people of the sun.
Tatted up, tatted up, tatted up, tatted up

Were here stay in your city, every day nitty gritty,
cause I don't got no papers you be saying it's a pity.

Play a mini concerto, serve your food at Roberto's,
should be in the Olympics, cause I jump so many
hurdles.

You call my kid an anchor baby, the government
can't save me, I get my thrills from your momma, so
she says call me, maybe.

We're the people, the people, the people of the sun.
Tatted up, tatted up, tatted up, tatted up

We're the people, the people, the people of the sun.
Tatted up, tatted up, tatted up, tatted up

We're the people, the people, the people of the sun.
Tatted up, tatted up, tatted up, tatted up

We're working hard breaking backs, we're stacking
up the racks, buying lots a ammo getting ready to
attack.

In the corner selling sacks, taking business from the blacks, then we even take they music even like a true wetback.

So don't be thinking just Beaner, took me straight to the cleaner, but at least he left money to buy me a chicken dinner.

We're the people, the people, the people of the sun. Tatted up, tatted up, tatted up, tatted up

We're the people, the people, the people of the sun. Tatted up, tatted up, tatted up, tatted up

We're the people, the people, the people of the sun. Tatted up, tatted up, tatted up, tatted up

We're neither here nor there, but really everywhere, were cruising in our Lolos, giving you a dirty stare.

You'll end up pricked like Nopales, drive you down to the valley, wrap you up in a carpet like chicken tamale, yea!

A return to Aztatlan, y la piel de mazapan, I bring my goods and my products from the hills of Culiacan.

We're the people, the people, the people of the sun. Tatted up, tatted up, tatted up, tatted up

We're the people, the people, the people of the sun. Tatted up, tatted up, tatted up, tatted up

We're the people, the people, the people of the sun. Tatted up, tatted up, tatted up, tatted up

A Tecate Revival

(Twenty-Four Hours Later)

The sun began to go down in Tecate, Baja California, a cozy little border town nestled between Mexicali and Tijuana with beautiful plazas and the best climate in the world; a literal paradise lost. A short, wiry, bespectacled old man sat behind the desk of the *Templo de Dios y Hermanos de Tecate* office, which was mostly empty except for the old man and his attorney, who was also his *compadre*; a few congregants prayed in the temple in the front building.

The door of the office was open. The whirling of an old ceiling fan could be heard in the background as flies hovered and flew around the area above the old man's head, which was buried in the books. A head peered inside the door. *"Buenas tardes, hola señores,"* Reymundo said as he waved one hand as if waiting for an invitation to come inside. *"Señores,* I noticed there's not a lot of people here, are you closed?" asked the big man of faith.

"No, the services are in the front," the old man stated as he pointed towards the temple.

"Yes, I know, I was just there. That's why I'm here," replied Reymundo. *"Señores,* I was passing through on my way to La Calera, you know, Sonora, you probably never heard of it, it's between Santa Ana and Hermosillo, Sonora, go *Naranjeros!"* He pumped his fists into the air to a quiet audience. "But you know, I notice you have a beautiful little picture-perfect town and I said to myself, Reymundo, you would do good to stay a while and soak in the sun, and well, I have no other skill but the gift of gab, and my word. You see, I was a preacher in a tiny little town in *el norte,* you probably never heard of it, yes? Well, I say this temple seemed deserving of Reymundo's attention, so here I am, ready to offer my services to you good *señores,"* he said.

"And what are those services?" said the old man. "I'm a preacher, *señor*, a shepherd to the People of the Sun. You have, what, fifteen people at your five o'clock evening Sunday service? You should be packed, *señores! Señores*, hire me as your preacher and I promise that within a month you will have one, two," Reymundo corrected himself, "three, no, five hundred people singing praises to the Lord, it will be standing room only, *señores*. And you know what that means, right, *señores*? More sheep, more offerings in the dish! Your cups will runneth over, *señores*. We'll have to hire more preachers and expand. Maybe into that abandoned warehouse next door." Reymundo pointed towards the empty warehouse, as if visually arranging the entire floor plan; gauging prospective parking. The men looked at each other befuddled, but not sure if they were being bullshitted.

Reymundo took the opportunity to slide into the middle of the room, knowing he had their full attention. He had them hooked; he could feel their hearts and read their souls. "*Señores*, give Reymundo a chance. I'm no good without a flock, and I promise you, I will lead them to greener pastures."

The two old guys sensed that they had better make the right decision, but they were cautious of the silver-tongued stranger. "What do you think, Cero?" the old man said to his attorney, who was also his *compadre*. The attorney, Cero, replied, "Sure, what harm can it do?"

Reymundo stood at the pulpit, raising his fists in the air. His audience was captivated. He yelled, he sang, he rhymed, and he danced. The packed house was surely standing room only; one month had passed and he was true to his word. Reymundo had completely changed the *Templo*, which had a new name now. Reymundo preached to the encouragement of the congregation.

"How many have to die before this government takes notice? They don't care for us because we are small, poor, uneducated; we are only important when it comes voting time, and oh, will they come in droves to get our votes. I say *ya basta*! Enough!" Reymundo mixed

English and Spanish to a bilingual congregation that seemed more in need of inspiration than anything else. A gospel choir broke out into song as children in angel costumes sang praises to the Lord. Ushers offered the congregants paper accordion-type fans to cool themselves off.

In the back office, a familiar gathering: The wiry old man, now in a slick blue suit, was talking with some concerned business leaders and some local clergy from the Catholic Church and the big Christian chapel. They were concerned about the activity going on; they were losing members to this church faster than the mercury rises during the Mexicali summer. "Sir, this man has a history. He is no good, and please, we beg you to consider our pleas before you lose everything. Something must be done." Father Lucas cried out to deaf ears; he had lost the spark of inspiration long ago and was only concerned with his own agenda.

The next day, Padre Reymundo sat in his office behind the temple; he sat in front of an old typewriter as he finished the last page of a manuscript. He looked at a Tijuana tabloid that had been opened to the crime section. He read out loud to himself from the middle of the article, written in Spanish. "Killed in the gunfire were Antonio Flores Hernandez, AKA *El Chapulin*, Jesus Campos Villaseñor, AKA *Chuyito*, and Eriberto Montiel Garibay, AKA Psyko." The last name got the old man teary eyed as he mumbled to himself, "Psyko, my friend, you were so close, but I guess you never had a chance. Rest in peace, young brother, rest in peace." Reymundo wiped his eyes as he sniffled a bit.

A few minutes later there was a knock on the door. It was an overnight courier. Reymundo told him to wait a couple minutes. Reymundo finished typing, removed the page with a zing and the sound of a bell, then lifted the Bible that sat atop the stack of typed pages and placed the page onto the two-inch stack. He placed them all into a large manila envelope, sealed it, wrote an address on the front and gave it to the courier with some money. The courier thanked Reymundo as he removed his cap, and then went on his way; the package was addressed to the *New York Times*.

A taxi arrived and a round woman with skinny legs, a pockmarked face and a strong back ran up to the Padre. She was crying, a happy cry. She hugged the big man as Reymundo paid for the taxi. He started introducing her to those coming towards him. "Rosa, *mucho gusto verte de Nuevo!*" Reymundo gushed over his friend; he puts his arm around her and walked her toward the chapel that had become his new home. He eagerly introduced her to anyone and everyone he encountered. Doña Rosa smiled and felt welcomed as they walked into the chapel.

A woman ran up to Reymundo. "Padre, padre, we are getting ready to start the service in the next twenty minutes, everything is set up, it looks beautiful." Padre Mundo walked into the chapel with Doña Rosa. He introduced her to a good looking woman about 30 years old. "This is Rosario Fuentes de Mendoza, she is the young lady whom Luis talked about, you know, when he first crossed into America. Chayo! This is Doña Rosa; she was with us on that day." Doña Rosa extended her hand. "Oh *si, mucho gusto*, you are exactly as Luis, rest in peace, described you," Doña Rosa said in Spanish. "Come on over here. You have to meet his parents. When they got my letter, they were more than happy to fly all the way over from Matamoros to celebrate with us, the last people who were with him," Padre Mundo said.

A poster-sized framed picture of Luis sat on an elaborately decorated Roman column surrounded by two floral arrangements on each side, up in the front of the chapel. The picture showed Luis mounted on a beautiful Andalusia horse in South Carolina, overlooking the Atlantic Ocean. The dates of his birth and death – which had occurred one month prior to the ceremony – were engraved on a small bronze plaque mounted on the lower part of the hand-carved cherry wood frame. The picture and a poem were sent by Marie Kimbo.

Next to the picture was another Roman column equally decorated which held an urn, the ashes of Luis, that had only recently been released by the authorities to the parents, who had made a special trip to Tijuana; they were happy that Reymundo had taken his time to perform a ceremony for their son, whose life was cut short in its prime; they knew their son and knew that what he did was on par with how he lived his life.

Nelly sat in the front, accompanied by Marty Silvers. She had been staying in Mexicali, where she would be attending the University of Baja California Mexicali in the fall, majoring in international law. Marty had confessed his love for her, but she had refused to take him up on his offer of marriage. She felt that if she were to marry it would be for love, not for convenience. He understood and was happy to spend any time with her; he had become her trusted confidante.

Doña Rosa grabbed the seat next to Nelly; they hugged and cried, then smiled and talked as the ceremony was about to begin. Reymundo stepped up to the podium, which was next to the picture and the urn. He put his hands on each side of the podium as if he were holding on for dear life. He put his head down for a moment; the whole chapel was silent. Reymundo raised his head and began to speak.

"I knew Luis for only one day, the last day of his life; a life cut short. However, in that day, I witnessed a tiny moment in time, like a twinkle of an eye. A moment which surely represented that which we should all strive to emulate. Luis lived a selfless life, a life full of love and support for anyone around him. He wasn't busy trying to make a million dollars, or trying to attain power. He did what he had loved to do as a child; he worked with horses.

"Luis went to the United States as a young man when he was 18 years old. He risked his life many times for his fellow man and woman. He loved the horses and they loved him back; he was amazing. He was truly his brother's keeper. He forgave those who did him wrong; he turned the other cheek.

"We will all miss him dearly. I will miss his spirit. He is in heaven riding a magnificent white horse with wings spread across the sky, and his sword of justice will cut into our hearts as a reminder that we must love each other as he has loved us.

"We don't have to be saintly or feel like we must carry the weight of the world on our shoulders. No, but shouldn't we be courteous, and supportive of anyone whom we encounter? We don't have to do wonders, but little everyday things add up to a good life. A simple hello to a stranger in a new town, a smile when we are cut off in traffic. Allowing a person to go ahead of us in a long line; paying for an old man's meal in secret. We don't have to save the world all at once, but we can save ourselves and allow God to save our souls."

(A poem written by a friend of Luis was sung by a group of young Hispanic rappers.)

> I see you riding in the sky, I'm feeling kind of sad, I
> wish it were another day, cause my brother died
> today
> Thinking I forgot of things you did for me, all the
> things you brought, I was too blind to see.
>
> Shoob shoob shooby doop
> Shoob shoob shooby doop
>
> You taught me life, to forget about strife, even help
> me save my marriage being nice to my wife
> All the things you did I could never repay ya, you
> were always there for me, so I wrote this little
> prayer.
>
> Shoob shoob shooby doop
> Shoob shoob shooby doop

In a million pieces you died a broken heart, every
time I hear this song, I think about your art.
Feeling kind of somber, I will always remember,
when I look up to the big blue sky, it's a daily
reminder

Shoob shoob shooby doop
Shoob shoob shooby doop

I guess I'll see ya, sooner than you know, I didn't
quite make it, on my way to the show
But I'm not sure if I'll go with angels, the way I
lived my life, probably going down below.

Shoob shoob shooby doop
Shoob shoob shooby doop

No more tears, or sad goodbyes, just the truth I
cannot lie,
Over my cold body my momma hovers
And then begins to cry.

Shoob shoob shooby doop
Shoob shoob shooby doop

As the service began to wind down, Reymundo was busying himself
with introducing everyone to everyone else. All of those who knew
Luis, the sensitive trainer of horses shared their stories. Some
laughed, some cried, others told bold tales of valiant galantry.

Reymundo hugged everyone and they all felt the comfort of the big
man's arms. Luis's mother and father, although saddened, were
happy to see such a display of affection and love towards their son; a
true sign of a life well lived.

As vehicles zoomed by outside on the street, some cars entered the parking lot which had filled up; the parking lot extended over two blocks. A car tire ran over a folding paper fan, and emblazoned across the face of the outstretched fan were the words:

"TEMPLO DEL MUNDO
Tecate, B.C. Mexico"

The paper fan was blown into the city street and rolled like a tumble weed into the future. A future full of uncertainty, but filled with the excitement of a man who had found his own promised land; a land of milk and honey, where his cup runneth over. A plaque placed over the front entrance of the chapel read, "If seven times I fell from grace, seven times I was forgiven."

The End- Fin

In Memory of

Ramona Osorio

Luis Ignacio Osorio

Victor Ayala Arizon

Francisco Alejandro Breton

Raymond "Aipa" Casias

&

All those who have died before reaching the American dream.

Descansen en paz Madre, hermano, sobrino, amigos, y paisanos.

(Rest in peace Mother, brother, nephew, friends, and countrymen)

A Special Thanks To

My wife Maria Guadalupe Morales de Osorio

Camila & Zoe Osorio (my beautiful granddaughters and inspiration)

eddieoradio.com

The Bear River Tribe

The Osorio Family of San Diego & Mexico

Miguel "Go Raiders" Sanchez

Linda Seed

The City of Tijuana, B.C. Mex. and Residencial del Bosque

The City of Angels – Los Angeles California

The City of San Diego, California – America's Finest City

City of Tecate B.C. Mexico

City of Lexington, Nebraska

International Association of Machinists

Rancho La Florida Santa Ana, Sonora Mexico

Rosarito, B.C. Mexico

The People of the Son Foundation

&

Amazon Online & Createspace.com

Author contact: dearlydeported2013@gmail.com

In association with

MundoWorld Productions

The Doctor Ed Show

and

www.eddieOradio.com

Library of Congress Control Number 2013905390

COPYRIGHT 2013 EDMUNDO OSORIO

MMXIII

www.ingramcontent.com/pod-product-compliance
Lightning Source LLC
Chambersburg PA
CBHW071254130626
46556CB00003B/1308